Just One Night

by

M.D. Alexander

All rights reserved. The reproduction of this work in whole or in part in any form by any electronic, mechanical, or other means, now known or hereafter invented, including xerography, recording, and photocopying, or in any information storage or retrieval system, is forbidden without the written permission of the author.

This is a work of fiction. All references to real places, people, or events are coincidental, and if not coincidental, are used fictitiously.

Copyright © 2022 M.D. Alexander
All rights reserved

Cover design by Covers in Color
www.coversincolor.com

ISBN: 9798428458534

M. D. ALEXANDER

Turning my passion for romance into pages

Dear readers,

Thank you for choosing Ethan and Aliyah's story. For those who have read #LIPS Vol 1 extended edition or subscribed to my newsletter, you may already be familiar with these two characters. For those who have not, I've included Aliyah and Ethan's short story as the prologue to provide a better reading experience for everyone.

Warning: *This book contains explicit language and descriptive sex scenes. (Some scenes include rough play) If this is an issue for you please do not read any further. If not, I hope you enjoy Aliyah and Ethan's story as much as I do.*

Happy reading!

M. D. Alexander

Acknowledgments

To my godmother,

You saw a 17-year-old girl catching two buses to work, and you cosigned for my first car. There's so much more to this story, but the bottom line is... At the time, I was a stranger to you. Thank you, DJ.

I love you!

Prologue

July~

Montego Bay, Jamaica~

"Ladies, we've arrived," Aliyah said. Along with her three best friends, she checked into The Grand Palace, a five-star resort in Montego Bay, Jamaica. Together, the four of them were about to embark on a six-day, five-night vacation.

"Okay, Aliyah, what's the first thing on our agenda? I know we have one," Amanda said as they followed the bellhop.

The other two women chuckled. Both knew she told the truth.

"Whatever. Don't throw shade at me because I'm organized."

Amanda remained quiet. She didn't want to turn their nice, friendly getaway into an argument. Also, there was the fact Aliyah paid for most of the trip.

As always, Tina spoke up, attempting to keep the peace. "I believe what Amanda is trying to ask is... What delightful things did you plan for us?"

"For today, nothing. I figured we would check in, change, and sit by the pool. Our adventure will start tomorrow."

Serena gave Aliyah a questionable stare. "Just what does our adventure consist of?"

With a grin, Aliyah went over the details. "Tomorrow, we're going zip-lining. On Tuesday, we'll go on a safari. On Wednesday, we'll go on the River's Fall tour..."

The three women looked on as she gave them the run-down of their entire itinerary. By the time they reached their rooms, Aliyah's talk about their upcoming adventures had exhausted them.

After changing, they headed toward the back of the hotel—an open floor plan with a spectacular view of the beach. Down by the pool, they found a table close to the bar.

"Do you guys realize, in less than two months, I'll be married!" Serena said.

Tina placed a hand on Serena's shoulder. "Oh sweetheart, you're not having second thoughts, are you?"

"What if she is? She needs to be certain she wants to get married. If she's having doubts, now is the chance to evaluate the situation," Aliyah said.

Amanda rolled her eyes at Aliyah's comment.

"No, I'm not having doubts. I love Nick," Serena assured.

"Then what's wrong?" Tina asked.

"Upstairs in the room, I realized how this might be our last trip together with the four of us. At least for a while."

Tina leaned over and hugged Serena. "I'm sure we'll still hang out like always."

"All right! Enough with the sappy stuff!"

As Aliyah's patience wore thin, the other three women stared at her. Although she appeared tough, they knew better.

"How about a round of drinks? On me?" Aliyah left the table and strolled in the bar's direction without waiting for a reply.

Ever since Serena announced her engagement, Aliyah tried to pretend it didn't bother her. Her irritation didn't come from jealousy, but from the fear of losing one of her dearest friends.

Aliyah loathed the idea of marriage. At twenty-seven, she was more concerned with money and how much she made. By the time she approached the bar, Aliyah had thought of every valid reason she would never get married.

"Hi, what can I get for you?" the bartender asked as he walked up to the other side.

"I'll take four *Bob Mar—*" Before Aliyah finished her order, a highly self-important man cut her off.

"Give me two bottles of *Patrón*," he ordered with authority.

Aliyah scanned over the man. He stood above average height, with fair skin, honey blonde hair, and brown eyes. His attire was expensive. She had no question about that. For his age, she figured him to be in his late twenties or early thirties. He was beyond handsome and smelled like the men's cologne section of a department store.

"Excuse Me! I was here first," Aliyah said, getting the man's attention.

From head to toe, his eyes roamed over her body, drinking her curves in before he spoke.

"Please forgive my rudeness." He glanced at the bartender. "Jeff, finish taking this beautiful woman's order first."

"Thanks." Aliyah turned away from the man's gaze. "Four *Bob Marley's*, please," she told Jeff.

"My name is Ethan. What's yours?"

"Aliyah," she said, trying not to make direct eye contact. When the bartender returned, she attempted to pay, but Ethan stopped her.

"I'll cover the bill. May I help you with those?"

"Oh. Yeah, sure." His actions stunned her. A simple apology was all she expected.

"How long are you here for?" Ethan asked, while

he walked beside her with two of the drinks.

"Six days. My friends and I are on a mini-vacation."

"Are you enjoying yourself so far?"

She met Ethan's gaze, and her stomach did a flip. "Yeah, I am."

When they reached the table, three sets of eyes studied them.

Amanda removed her shades. "Aliyah, who's your friend?"

"This is Ethan. He was kind enough to buy our drinks and help me bring them over." Aliyah looked back at him. "Thank you again."

"You're quite welcome. I hope you and your friends continue to enjoy the rest of your stay." Ethan turned toward the others. "Ladies," he said with emphasis, then walked away.

Tina hit Aliyah on the shoulder. "Liya!"

"What?"

"So you're gonna let that sexy man walk away?"

"What else am I supposed to do?"

"Get his number! Do something!" Serena said.

"His Number? Have you two forgotten we are in Jamaica? Also, we're here to have fun as a group and not hook up with strangers. Even if they do—damn, he *is* fine, isn't he?"

All three women nodded yes.

Amanda took a sip of her drink and smacked her

lips. "Better you than me. I could use a little vanilla in my life."

The four of them burst into laughter.

"I hear that." Aliyah focused her attention toward the direction Ethan walked. A small part of her hoped she ran into him again.

"What do you mean, we're not on the schedule? I secured and paid for this trip months ago." Aliyah scowled at the concierge behind the counter as he typed on the keyboard.

"I'm sorry, but we've booked our manifest until Saturday."

"That won't work. My friends and I will be on a flight heading back to Seattle."

"Would you like a rain-check for another date?"

"No. I want a refund, and I want to speak with your manager."

"What's the problem?"

Aliyah turned around to find Ethan behind her. She didn't know how long he stood there, but she detected genuine concern on his face.

"Hi."

"Good morning." Ethan lifted his chin toward the desk. "What's going on?"

"I booked a zip line tour when I made the room reservations. They didn't have enough seats available for the dates I requested. Instead of informing me, they allowed me to complete the reservation and pay for the tour. Now that we're here, they can't accommodate us."

"Give me a minute," Ethan said. He placed a reassured touch on Aliyah's shoulder, took his cell phone out, and approached the concierge desk.

Aliyah stood by and waited as he spoke with the clerk. She noticed Ethan's presence had the man on pins and needles. Behind her, Aliyah glimpsed at the two gentlemen that stood against the wall. They dressed in black suits, and both wore dark shades. The secret service came to mind as she looked them over.

"All taken care of," Ethan said as he returned. "A van will be here in forty-five minutes to take you and your friends on the zip-lining tour."

"Wow! Um, thank you," she said, struggling to find her words.

"My pleasure."

"Well, I better go inform the others."

"Yes, of course. Enjoy your day." Ethan flashed her another quick smile before he joined the two men and proceeded outside.

"Who in the hell are you?" Aliyah mumbled to herself as she re-approached the desk. "Excuse me. Is he the manager?"

"Oh, no, ma'am. Mr. Phillips owns the resort."

Aliyah's eyes widened. Things suddenly made sense.

"Thanks."

After rounding up everyone, Aliyah returned to the lobby to find a Mercedes-Benz commercial van waiting for them at the curb. The inside came stocked with drinks, snacks, and a mini-bar.

"Damn, Liya, this is some top-of-the-line shit! How much did all this cost?" Serena plundered through the snacks as she waited for an answer.

Aliyah told them about the incident with their reservation and how Ethan stepped in. She also informed them he owned the resort.

Serena wore the same expression on her face Aliyah did when she found out. "Are you serious!"

"Yep."

"Not only is the man sexy as hell, but he's also rich. If you don't fuck him, I will," Amanda said.

The sound of the driver choking made them all glance toward the front.

"Do you think he heard me?"

"We all heard you, Amanda," Tina said.

When they returned from their tour, most of the day had vanished. Aliyah doubted their experience would have been the same if they'd gone with the others as planned. Her mishap turned out to be a blessing in disguise. To top things off, she received an email notifying her of a refund.

First thing in the morning, Aliyah planned to speak with Ethan about the situation. She didn't expect to be refunded since they had gotten to go on the tour.

The following day, Aliyah stopped by the concierge desk before she and the others headed out on the safari tour.

"May I help you?" the clerk behind the desk asked.

"Yes. I wondered if Mr. Phillips might be available."

"Mr. Philips?"

"Yes, the owner."

"Oh, I'm aware of who he is. However, I'm afraid he doesn't see anyone without an appointment."

"Right, how silly of me. Do you have a sheet of paper you can spare?"

The woman gave Aliyah a sheet from the fax machine. "Is this sufficient?"

"Perfect." Aliyah scribbled down her message, then handed the paper back to the clerk. "Can you make sure he gets this?"

"Yes, ma'am. I will."

"Thanks."

The next evening, after a long day filled with wine sampling and swimming, they returned to the resort. Drained, all four women migrated to Aliyah's room.

"I never realized fun could be so exhausting," Tina said.

Knocks at the door interrupted the group's laughter; but neither attempted to answer.

Aliyah looked over at them. "Please, don't everyone stand at once."

"This *is* your room," Amanda said.

With a sarcastic smile, Aliyah moved to toward the door. "Who is it?"

"Room service. I have a message for Ms. Aliyah Carter."

Aliyah opened the door. "I'm Ms. Carter."

The bellhop handed the envelope over.

"Thank you."

When Aliyah turned around, the others studied her with fascination.

"Oh, now you care who's at the door?"

Aliyah opened the envelope and scanned over the letter. When she saw Ethan's name, she became intrigued.

"Based on the grin plastered across your face, I'm guessing the message is from Ethan," Amanda said.

Aliyah nodded and read the contents more in-depth.

Ms. Carter,

I apologize for taking so long to respond to your message. I hope you and your friends enjoyed yourselves. As for the refund, it's policy and procedure; therefore, my hands are tied. On another note, I recall you stating you were only here for a few days. If you don't have plans, I would like to invite you to dinner tomorrow night?

Please call me at the number below. I look forward to hearing from you.

Sincerely,

Ethan Phillips (876-555-5555).

After reading, Aliyah walked into the bedroom and closed the door.

All three women ran and placed their ears against

it.

Aliyah sat on the side of the bed and dialed Ethan's number.

"Hello."

"Ethan, it's Aliyah. I got your message, and I accept your invitation."

"Great, I can't wait to see you again."

The notion of him longing for her excited Aliyah. "For tomorrow, is there a certain dress code I should consider?"

"Casual is fine. So, how has this visit to Jamaica been treating you?"

"Excellent. I owe an extra thank you to this one gentleman."

"Oh?"

"Perhaps I could thank him before I leave. Unless he objects to the idea."

"I'm sure he'd like that."

"What time should I be ready?"

"How does five o'clock sound?"

"I'll be here."

"See you tomorrow."

"Okay. Bye."

After hanging up the phone, Aliyah walked over to the bedroom door and opened it. Amanda, Tina, and Serena stood in the doorway. She shook her head and pushed past them.

"What's the deal? Are you meeting up with Mr.

Sexy or not?" Amanda asked.

Aliyah stalled with her response as she opened the refrigerator. "Maybe."

Tina and Serena gave each other a hi-five.

"My girl is about to get her groove back," Amanda said.

Aliyah sucked her teeth. "I never lost it."

In unison, Tina and Serena shrieked with laughter.

That morning, Aliyah stayed in bed. Trees slightly obstructed her view of the ocean, yet still, the scene created a beautiful backdrop. Due to their constant activities, this was the first time she allowed herself to appreciate it. As she waited for the time to pass, she imagined what a night with Ethan would consist of. She couldn't deny her attraction to him, even when he skipped her in line.

Beyond his looks, she found his take-charge attitude alluring. He was a powerful and wealthy man, which she considered a plus.

At a quarter to five, the phone in her room buzzed. Ethan called and said he was ten minutes away. Attired in her orange mini chiffon dress, Aliyah was ready to go.

When knocks at the door came, she grabbed her small chain-linked purse and walked over to answer it.

"My, my, my. You are exquisite," Ethan complimented.

"Thank you."

As they walked down the hall, Ethan held her hand and continued to hold it inside the elevator. Once they arrived at the first floor, Aliyah imagined he would release her. She figured he wouldn't want the staff to associate him with a guest. She had been wrong. Ethan never let go of her hand. Not until they stepped outside, and he assisted her inside his S Class Mercedes-Benz 500 coupe.

They drove for at least an hour until the only thing visible was acres of open land. Finally, they pulled into a Mediterranean Mansion's driveway. Aliyah waited as Ethan came around and assisted her out of the car. Together, they walked toward the entrance. A breathtaking view of the ocean caught her attention, reminding her of the lobby at the resort.

"We'll be having dinner outside tonight. Is that all right?"

Aliyah turned her gaze toward him. "Are you

kidding me? That sunset looks amazing! Of course, it is."

Ethan led her to the back of the mansion and then outside.

While they strolled down the path, Aliyah paid attention to the details. Such as the Tiki lights that lit the way, the table set for two with the chef standing by, and the soft music that played in the background. Aliyah doubted she was the first woman Ethan had seduced, but she damn sure considered herself special.

"Good evening Mr. Phillips and Ms. Carter."

"Evening, Tim."

Aliyah waved and gave a friendly smile. "What's for dinner?" she asked as Ethan helped her into the chair.

"Shrimp and steak Kabobs."

"Sounds delicious."

Over dinner, they talked about the various sites Aliyah and her friends visited while in Montego Bay. She was glad their conversation remained casual. Aliyah preferred not to get too personal. She didn't plan on seeing Ethan after that night.

"Ready for dessert?"

"Yes, I have a little room left."

"Don't worry; it's light." Ethan winked at her. "I'll be right back."

Soon, he returned with chocolate fondue, and a tray filled with strawberries.

"Where's your Chef?"

"He's gone for the night."

"So, we're alone?"

"Yes." Ethan moved his chair closer to her and dipped a strawberry into the chocolate before bringing it to her lips.

Aliyah opened her mouth and took a bite. "Yummy."

"Is it? Let me have a taste." Ethan leaned forward. He sucked her bottom lip before his tongue slipped inside her mouth. "Mmm, you're right, it is." With his hand still on her chin, Ethan stared into her eyes. "I want to be clear and upfront with you. I brought you here with every intention of fucking you."

The corners of Aliyah's mouth turned upward. "I came here with every intention of letting you."

With a chuckle, Ethan sat back in his chair. He sensed she was used to being in control. "I must warn you; I play rough."

Aliyah stood and picked up her glass. "I'll be over by the pool when you're ready." She gave Ethan a wink, then strutted toward the canopy bed.

Amused by her cockiness, he remained in his seat and observed as she undressed.

Despite a slight buzz, Aliyah drank the rest of her wine. She glanced over her shoulder and blew Ethan a kiss before lying on the bed.

Not wanting to keep her waiting, he joined her.

At the foot of the bed, Ethan became engrossed in Aliyah's beautiful body. His dick throbbed while he impatiently waited to be inside of her.

"Show me how you make yourself cum."

Aliyah's eyes widened.

"What? Surely you're not shy."

"No, I'm not."

"Show me."

Aliyah accepted his challenge. She licked two fingers and rubbed them against her clit. With her other hand, she squeezed her breast and pinched her nipples.

A satisfied moan escaped when she found her rhythm. Fueled by her own administration of pleasure, she bit down on her lip and moved her fingers faster. The reality of masturbating in front of Ethan aroused her. The embarrassment she once felt had disappeared. After sliding her fingers inside, she opened her legs wider, giving him a better view.

Ethan licked his lips and rubbed the print of his dick. "Show me how you want me to fuck you?"

He studied Aliyah while he undressed. From the sounds of sexual gratification she made, he suspected she was close. Once naked, Ethan stroked his dick while she came.

"Very good, but I'm sure I can get you wetter.

Turn over."

Ethan climbed inside the bed and lifted her ass. He knew her clit was sensitive, so he rubbed his hands against it. As he spread her thighs, he stuck his face between them, shoving his tongue deep inside her.

A shiver moved through Aliyah when Ethan flicked her clit and sucked. She jerked when his hand came down on her ass, and his fingers replaced his tongue.

"Mmm," she whined when he rotated them and smacked her ass. Unable to hold back any longer, her cries echoed against the sky as she came again.

Ethan didn't give Aliyah time to recover. While behind her, he grabbed her waist and sat her on his lap, driving his entire length inside her.

"Oh, fuck!" she screamed as he held her in place and rolled his body against hers. Aliyah had never been in that position before. It took her by surprise when he gripped her arms and fucked her harder.

"My dick feels amazing, doesn't it?" he boasted, causing her body to bounce out of control.

"Yes!"

Ethan took delight in making her ass jiggle. At the risk of coming too soon, he let go of her hands and fucked her slower.

Aliyah became powerless underneath him. Sounds of pleasure oozed from her mouth as they moved as one.

After a few more thrusts, he pulled out. "Lay on your back."

She did as he instructed. When they locked eyes, Aliyah became afraid. Not of him hurting her, but of him possessing her.

Ethan parted her thighs and slid back inside of her. "Lock your legs around my waist." Once she secured her legs, Ethan wrapped his hands around her neck.

Automatically, she reached for them.

"Relax, I won't hurt you."

With uncertainty, she placed her hands on the bed.

Ethan thrust inside her, and with each thrust, he squeezed her throat.

Aliyah couldn't comprehend the way her body responded.

"Your pussy is so wet. You belong to me tonight."

She nodded, unable to speak, as his strokes became more aggressive and his hands tightened. Aliyah struggled to breathe, but she loved every minute.

"Are you about to come?"

Again, she shook her head yes.

"Good girl."

Seconds later, Aliyah gasped for air as her pussy squeezed his dick and her juices soaked the sheets.

Satisfied, Ethan removed his hands from around her neck. He pulled out and erupted on her stomach.

"Next time, I'm going to come inside you."

Too busy catching her breath, Aliyah laid in bed exhausted. She watched as he got up and disappeared. Moments later, he returned with a towel in his hand. She remained still as he used the warm cloth to clean her.

"Will you stay with me tonight?" he implored, once finished.

"My plane leaves at eight o'clock tomorrow morning."

Ethan nodded and stroked the side of her face.

On the drive back to the resort, neither said a word. After parking, Ethan turned off the car and reached to open his door.

"What are you doing?" Aliyah asked.

Ethan looked at her with confusion. "I was going to walk you up to your room."

"No, you don't need to do that." Aliyah reached for her door and pulled on the latch, but Ethan stopped her.

"Wait," he said, touching her shoulder. "Maybe —"

Aliyah brought her finger up to his lips. "We shared one night; let's not ruin the evening with promises we don't intend to keep." She leaned over and kissed his lips. "Goodbye, Ethan." Without a second glance, she stepped out of his car and disappeared inside.

September~

Seattle, Washington

Aliyah fished inside her purse, searching for something to ease her headache. As the chief project manager for Mills Architectural & Design, she oversaw three major projects.

"Hey Aliyah, do you have a second?" Her boss and friend Michael Callaway tapped on the door before he walked into her office.

"No, but that's never stopped you."

"Can you please do me a favor?" He put his hands together in the praying position.

Aliyah found it hilarious how he acted like she had a choice. "What is it?"

"I have an important prospective client coming." Michael checked his watch. "He'll be here in less than thirty minutes."

Aliyah knew where their little chat headed.

"I need you to work your magic and win him over. If you land this project, I'll give you a month off."

She and Michael both knew he would never give her a month off. Still, she didn't call him out.

"Please! You're the only one I trust. Anyone else might screw this up."

"Don't you remember? You've already assigned me to three other *important* clients."

"I know, but this one is more important. So important, I'll reassign the other projects to someone else."

"All three?"

"Yes, all three."

Aliyah sighed. "You don't have to reassign all three, just one."

"So, does that mean you'll do it?"

"Yes. I'll meet you in the conference room in fifteen minutes."

Michael mouthed the words "Thank you" and left her office.

After taking some ibuprofen, Aliyah stopped by the bathroom, then headed toward the conference room.

"Aliyah." Danita, from marketing, called her name.

"Yeah, what's up?"

"Have you seen the client walking around with Michael?"

"No, not yet."

"Girl, that man is beyond fine. It should be a crime to be that sexy."

"Damn, he's that cute?"

"The word cute is an insult to him." Danita fanned her hand. "With my luck, he's gay."

Aliyah flashed her brows. "Well, I'm on the way to meet with him now. I'll give you my verdict when I come back." With a chuckle, Aliyah continued in the conference room direction.

The moment she stood at the door, she breathed in *his* scent. Aliyah peeked through the glass window, needing to be sure. When she saw Ethan sitting at the table, it felt like someone hit her in the stomach with a sledgehammer.

She squeezed her eyes shut. Aliyah had two choices. Pretend she didn't know Ethan and hope he played along. Or acknowledge him and deal with questions from everyone. She went with the first option.

"Come on, Aliyah, you got this." She put on her game face, then pushed the door to the conference room open.

The second she walked in the door, Ethan stood to his feet.

"Ah, here she is now," Michael said. "Mr. Phillips, I'd like you to meet our chief project manager, Aliyah Carter."

"I'm pleased to meet you, Mr. Phillips." Aliyah extended her hand.

Ethan accepted, but held on longer and tighter than needed. "The pleasure is all mine, Ms. Carter. I'm glad you could join us."

For the entire duration of the meeting, Ethan's eyes burned a hole through Aliyah.

She, on the other hand, kept her attention aimed at Michael.

"Is there anything else you would like to add, Aliyah?" Michael asked.

Only then did she look at Ethan. "Here at Mills Architectural & Design, we work hard to maintain our client's vision throughout the entire process. We also understand how important staying on budget is, so we don't make any changes until consulting with you."

"Say no more, Ms. Carter. I'm all yours."

Aliyah swallowed. Well aware, he referred to something else. She shifted her attention to Michael. He wore a wide grin on his face, oblivious to what was going on.

"I'll let you two gentlemen work out the details." Aliyah stood to leave.

"Ms. Carter? Do you have a number where I can contact you?"

Aliyah reached into her planner and pulled one of her business cards out. "Here you go, Mr. Phillips." She forced herself not to show emotion while she handed it to him. Their fingers brushed, and Aliyah instantly craved his touch. She turned around and took two steps when Ethan spoke again.

"Is this your office number?"

Aliyah faced him. "Yes."

"I'll also need your personal number. In case I make any sudden changes, you should be made aware of."

Bullshit! That's what Aliyah thought. But she remained professional and wrote her cell number on the back of the card she gave him.

"Thank you, Ms. Carter. I'll be in touch."

Aliyah walked out into the hall. She took several deep breaths, then headed toward her office.

"So, what's the verdict?" Danita whispered when Aliyah passed by.

"Definitely gay."

"Dammit!" Danita cursed under her breath.

Aliyah continued in the direction of her office. She'd barely made it inside before her phone chimed. She didn't need to read the text to know who it was from.

Chapter One

What was Ethan doing in Seattle? Aliyah asked herself that question moment she inhaled his expensive cologne. Out of all the Architectural companies, why Mills? Had Ethan tracked her there?

Aliyah groaned in despair as she sat behind the large maple-wood desk inside her corner office. "No, why would he do that?" She reached for her planner, and a sudden knock at the door summoned Aliyah's attention. Prepared to see Ethan's face, she straightened her back and put up her defenses. "Come in."

Her shoulders relaxed the moment Michael entered. She noted the victorious expression from the conference room remained engraved on his face.

"I must say, I've never witnessed you work your magic so fast." Michael peered at Aliyah with interest. "Why do I get the impression you and

Ethan Phillips have met already?"

Aliyah considered admitting the truth, but she would have to answer questions she wasn't ready to address herself. "No. I've never seen him before today." She kept her head lowered; and, with surprising ease, typed as though her thoughts weren't disheveled.

"What's wrong? You seem upset," Michael questioned as he moved closer.

"I have a slight headache. I took something a while ago, but it hasn't kicked in yet. ... Is there anything else?" Aliyah asked, when Michael continued to watch her oddly.

"No."

"Well, if you don't mind."

Aliyah's not-so-subtle way of kicking Michael out hadn't gone unnoticed.

"You do remember I'm your boss?" he replied with a humorous tone.

Aliyah waved her hand over the stack of papers on her desk. "How could I forget?"

"Oh, right," Michael remembered his earlier promise and took out his cell phone. "I need to reassign those other projects to McCallister. I'm sure Mr. Phillips is going to keep you busy."

Buzz. Buzz. Buzz.

Aliyah's eyes darted toward her phone. The name displayed, caused her stomach to plunge.

"Are you going to get that?" Michael pressed.

"Yes." With the sincerest smile, she could form, Aliyah answered her phone. "Hello, Mr. Phillips. Nice to hear from you so soon."

"Why didn't you respond to my text? I expect a lot more proficiency from you, Ms. Carter."

"One moment, sir." Aliyah removed the phone from her ear and eyed Michael. "You're supposed to be calling McCallister, remember?"

Suspiciously, Michael nodded and left.

Aliyah placed the phone back against her ear. "We need to talk."

"You took the words out of my mouth, Buttercup. How about dinner tonight?"

The baritone in his voice made Aliyah's head swim with arousal. She brought a hand to her neck and pressed her thighs together. *Dammit! Why am I letting him affect me like this?*

"Is that a, yes?"

"Ethan, this is my—"

"It'll be a business dinner."

Aliyah remained quiet as she debated with herself. She hadn't been given the chance to construct a well-thought-out speech, and was uncertain of how to proceed.

"Hello? Are you still there?"

"Fine," she reluctantly said. "Where is this *business* dinner going to take place?"

"There's an excellent restaurant on the roof of Emerald Plaza. Have you heard of it?"

The sureness in his voice caused a roll of Aliyah's eyes. Everyone knew the restaurant he spoke of was top of the line. For Ethan to secure a last-minute reservation there meant he had connections. "Yes, Aromas."

"Perfect! I'll set our reservation for seven. Is that okay for you?"

"Yes."

"See you then, Buttercup."

Aliyah ended the call. She shook her head at the pet name he'd given her. "Why Buttercup? This can't be good."

She hated the flutters that formed in her stomach. She didn't want to like the pet name, but Aliyah couldn't suppress her arousal. And despite her self-discipline, she couldn't resist her attraction to Ethan.

Checkmate. Ethan smirked at his minor victory. He hadn't intended on ruffling Aliyah's feathers, but he needed to break through her composed demeanor. The woman had actually sat across from him and pretended not to know him.

What were the odds of Aliyah living in Seattle and working for the architect company he'd sought-after for his new ski resort? Ethan could have looked her address up. He'd contemplated it but didn't, for the sake of respecting her privacy and not appearing like a stalker.

As his driver, Todd, navigated through the streets of downtown Seattle, Ethan glanced at the tall sky-scraping buildings in passing. The feelings that brewed inside of him were new. He never thought a one-night-stand would leave him so incomplete and craving more. To say he desired Aliyah was an understatement. His yearning for her had become an unattainable nuisance.

Although Ethan preferred one-night stands, that was not the case with Aliyah. He wanted more from her, more than she wanted to give. Now, by some twisted fate, she was accessible, just not available. To make matters worse, she maintained the same coldness she did when she stepped out of his car and told him to fuck off without uttering the words.

At the realization, Ethan grunted in frustration.

"Is everything okay, sir?"

"Yes, Todd. Disregard any of my obscenities or loud sounds. I'm thinking."

Todd chuckled and nodded.

Ethan resumed his assessment of the situation. Why the hell was she so content with one night?

Perhaps that wasn't her first time. Like a disease, more unsettling thoughts crept into his mind.

Did Aliyah do this often? Was there a long list of men she had slept with and walked away from? If so, Ethan vowed to be her last.

With that in mind, he set the wheels in motion and called Aromas. Since he and the owner, Peter Wright, were college buddies and the restaurant was inside Ethan's hotel, last-minute reservations weren't an issue.

"Aromas, Rebecca speaking."

"Hi, Rebecca, this is Ethan Phillips. I'd like to make a reservation for seven in the La Cache dining room."

"Yes, sir. No problem. We'll have your table ready when you arrive."

"Thank you." Ethan hung up, and his mind resumed its endless wonder about Aliyah. "Soon, Buttercup. I'll tear down every wall you've built and erase every man you've had. When I'm done, you'll be mine. All mine."

Knock, knock.

"Michael, if you keep barging in here, I won't get any work done."

"Sorry, it's me," Danita announced.

"Oh, hey. Come in."

Danita sat on the chaise by the large window and peered down at the people who'd taken on a miniature form. "Is it true you can kill someone by dropping a penny from this high up?" she asked.

Aliyah raised a brow. "I wouldn't know. I try not to make a habit of dropping pennies from tall buildings. ... Are you all right?"

"Yeah." Danita continued to stare out the window. "You really think he's gay?"

"Gay? Who's gay?"

"What do you mean, who? Ethan Phillips!"

Aliyah had forgotten the vicious little lie she'd said in the heat of the moment. She knew if she didn't recount her statement ASAP, by noon, everyone in the office building would think Ethan was gay—courtesy of Danita. Ethan may have been a reminder of her lack of self-control, but Aliyah didn't want others to believe something that wasn't true. "I lied."

"I knew it!" Danita tilted her head to the side. "You were saving him for yourself, weren't you?"

"Please! I don't want him."

"In that case, do you think I have a chance?"

Aliyah stared at Danita. "Why would you be interested in him when you have a boyfriend?"

Surprise flashed in Danita's eyes. "Who says I'm dating anyone?"

"You did. The other day when you went to the movies, and the night before that when you had dinner at Vendemmia."

With unease, Danita shifted on the chaise.

As bad as Aliyah wanted to laugh, she held it in. Danita had never told her either of those things. Michael had, but only after Aliyah cornered him and made him come clean.

Over a month ago, Aliyah had seen the two exchange a few heated glances. She suspected something but wasn't sure until she caught Danita sneaking out of Michael's office and confirmed her suspicion. Despite Danita's interest in Ethan, Aliyah knew different. It was a deflection to divert suspicion away from her and Michael's secret relationship.

Aliyah hadn't been the only one who thought they had something going on. Rumors had been circulating ever since the two arrived to work together.

"I don't remember telling you that," Danita said with uncertainty.

"Oh, I must have you mixed up with someone else."

Like Michael, Aliyah considered Danita a friend.

Although she'd known Michael longer, Aliyah thought for sure Danita would have felt comfortable enough to confide in her.

Danita stood. "I had a spreadsheet due yesterday. I better go finish."

"Sure. Although we both know you have nothing to worry about."

With an unspoken awkwardness, Danita walked out of the office.

At once, Aliyah felt horrible. There she was, trying to pry the truth out of Danita but refusing to be truthful about Ethan.

Ding!

Not again. Aliyah peeked at the text that came through her phone. Relief eased her anxiety.

Amanda:
Want to meet tonight?
Received: 11:30am.

Aliyah couldn't simply say no. Amanda would press on and want an explanation.

Aliyah:
I can't tonight.
I'm meeting with a client.
How about tomorrow?
Delivered: 11:31 am

For the moment, Aliyah deemed it necessary to

keep Ethan's presence in Seattle a secret.

Amanda:
Tomorrow is fine. I'll inform the others.
Received: 11:32 am

Aliyah:
Thanks. I'll text you tomorrow.
Delivered: 11:33am

Since high school, the four women had been close. They gave each other crap from time to time, often joking about their different backgrounds and ethnicities. Yet still, they were the three best friends Aliyah could have asked for. Despite her worries before Serena's wedding, nothing had changed. The group continued to meet up for their weekly dinners and impromptu gatherings.

At six-forty-five, Aliyah entered the Emerald Plaza. She walked across the Italian porcelain tiled floor of the lobby toward the elevators. Inside, she pressed the button for Aromas. As the elevator ascended, she took a few deep breaths. No matter how much she desired Ethan, she intended to keep their relationship strictly business.

She refused to let his mesmeric brown eyes convince her otherwise. Aliyah stepped off the elevator with her mind made and strolled toward the hostess.

"Hi. I believe my party is here."

"What's the name?" The petite brunette's eyes shifted to the guest list as she waited for Aliyah's answer.

"Phillips."

The woman's head lifted abruptly. "Oh, right this way."

Aliyah followed as the hostess led her into an exclusive part of the restaurant, sealed off by a set of tall black marble accented doors. She waited as the woman held them open for her.

"Thank you," Aliyah said, noting the small round dining table inside the room—occupied by Ethan.

"Good evening, Buttercup."

He spoke with calmness. Too calm. "Good evening," Aliyah reciprocated, hoping to match his tone. After all, this was a battle of wits, and she played to win.

Ethan stood and walked around the table. "Please have a seat." He pulled out the chair and motioned for Aliyah to sit.

With much restraint, she ignored the tingle that crept up her spine. "Thanks."

"My pleasure."

An eternity seemed to pass while they sat in silence. Aliyah parted her lips to speak, but a server entered, causing her to remain quiet. As he poured the red liquid into their glasses, Aliyah lost herself in a daydream. She almost forgot every valid thought and sound reason not to involve herself with Ethan.

"What's on your mind, Buttercup?" Ethan asked once the server disappeared.

Heat filled Aliyah's cheeks as his gaze lingered on her. She felt exposed, as if private thoughts displayed across her forehead. Like most people—when put on the spot—she became defensive. "Why are you here, Ethan?"

"Here, as in Seattle?"

"Yes."

"Why do you think I'm here, Aliyah?"

Just hearing her name on his tongue sent a bolt of electricity through her, but Aliyah couldn't reveal that. "I'm not sure. That's why I'm asking."

"I live here," Ethan said with a shrug.

Aliyah cast her eyes downward. "I didn't know."

"How could you? The last time we were in each other's presence, you didn't care to stick around for small talk."

Aliyah figured their night together would come up, but Ethan's bitter tone was a surprise. "I'm not sure what you want from me."

"I'm certain you do. I'm even positive you want it, too."

"Oh?" Aliyah noticed a faint tremor in her hand when she picked up her wine glass. "I hate to burst your bubble, but I don't have the slightest idea of what you're talking about."

"You're lying."

"Excuse me?"

"Your sweet lips deny the truth, but that body of yours tells me a different story."

Aliyah's eyes widened.

"And judging from the way you're staring at me now, I'd say you're embarrassed that I'm aware you share my opinion of a better use for this table."

"Such as?" Aliyah bit back. Her pride wouldn't let Ethan see her sweat.

"Me, bending you over it and fucking you the way you need to be."

You had to ask. Mentally, she chastised herself for provoking him. "Listen, Ethan—"

He held up his hand. "However, if you insist on sticking to our businesslike relationship, I'll have to respect that, for now." He pushed a manila folder across the table.

"What's this?"

"The contract your boss, Michael, prepared. I told him I'd return it through you."

With the heightened sense of hightailing it out of there, Aliyah picked up the folder and scooted her chair back.

"Where are you going?"

"Our meeting is over, correct?"

Ethan leaned forward. His voice took on a smoother tone. "Stay for dinner."

Don't do it. Aliyah forced herself to maintain eye contact as she battled her thoughts. The sound of the server returning gave her an excuse to look away, but Ethan's voice called her attention once more.

"Please, sit down. It's just dinner."

"I'm learning nothing is ever *just* with you."

Ethan chuckled. "Fair enough."

As Aliyah eased back into her seat, she held Ethan's gaze. At that very moment, she realized, if, given a chance, he'd own her.

Ethan increased the speed of his treadmill. Sweat dripped down his body, and his heart rate continuously climbed. He needed to think. He always did his best thinking when he ran, so he kept the pace. Aliyah Carter was in Seattle. No matter how many times Ethan told himself that, he struggled to believe it.

He wondered what evil dimension he'd warped into. No woman ever pretended not to know him. Nor did he negotiate with them, at least not with relationships and sex. Aliyah was driving him crazy.

Despite her business-only attitude, she wanted him as much as he wanted her.

The tiny spark of electricity he felt when she handed him her card was nothing compared to her body language at Aromas. She would be his. Hell, she already was. He just needed to convince her to accept the truth.

Ethan slowed the treadmill until it stopped. After he grabbed the towel and his phone, he stepped down. He dried his face, then scrolled through his contacts as he walked over to the bench in his home gym. While controlling his breaths, he located Michael's number and pressed the call button.

"Michael, this is Ethan Phillips."

"Mr. Phillips. How can I help you?"

"I want to schedule a visit to the site. Can we meet in your office tomorrow morning at seven-thirty to discuss the details?"

"Sure. Seven-thirty is fine."

"Good. See you then."

Ethan headed toward his bedroom and into the master bath. He removed the drenched black T-shirt and shorts, then stepped into the shower. With his mind in a fog, he remained unbothered by the streams of cold water that sprinkled onto his flesh before the temperature adjusted.

Like every night for the last two months, the vision of Aliyah's naked body joined him in the shower. For the millionth time, he pictured his hand wrapped around her neck while the other held her leg, and he viciously plowed into her. Without hesitation, Ethan grabbed his swollen shaft that begged for release.

"That's it, Buttercup, take all of me." Seconds later, he reached his climax. The thought of Aliyah's tight walls milking him dry made him cum hands-free.

"Fuck!" Ethan groaned when his hot seed shot out and splashed against the tile.

As the water washed away the evidence, Aliyah's face remained. He thought about the way she moaned and whimpered when he hit her G-spot. The way her eyes rolled in the back of her head when she came. Instantly, Ethan became hard again.

"What the hell is this? My dick stays harder than a teenage boy going through puberty." He leaned his forehead against the cold marble tile, and his eyes darted toward his erection.

He could either relieve himself once more; or go to bed with blue balls. He made the wiser choice. Only this time, as he glided his hand back and forth, he imagined Aliyah's mouth wrapped around the tip.

As one hand pumped and the other braced the wall, he cursed the woman responsible for his constant confusion and a relentless hard-on.

Chapter Two

*I*t had been a long drive home for Aliyah, and after a night filled with dreams of her trip to Montego Bay, she awakened restlessly. Through heavy eyelids, she peeked at the folder on her nightstand. From the other side of the bed, she grabbed a pillow and pressed her face into it.

Despite Ethan's cordial behavior toward the end of their evening, it had done little to quiet her nerves. When they left the restaurant, and his hand covered the small of her back, she damn near jumped out of her skin.

"Grrr!" Aliyah groaned, becoming more irritated. She hated to admit that Ethan did things to her libido, but she wouldn't cave. Not if she wanted to remain sane or keep everyone at her job out of her private life.

Two years had passed since she dated and a year

since she had sex. Aliyah had sworn off any type of romantic or sexual relationship until 'that' night. Somehow, Ethan broke through her defenses. The one time—in a long time—she'd allowed herself freedom had backfired.

"One damn night."

In irritation—toward herself—she tossed the pillow aside, then did the same with her fluffy comforter, before hopping out of bed.

He's just a man. Aliyah repeated inside her head on the way to her bathroom. *Yeah, a man who gave you the best sex of your life. Not to mention the most intense orgasms you've ever experienced.*

In mid-stride, Aliyah stopped and squeezed her eyes shut. Already, insanity reared its ugly head.

After bumbling through her morning routine and engaging in a not so delightful heart-to-heart with herself, Aliyah called her mother. She'd recently had her gallbladder removed and was recovering.

"Hey, mom. How are you feeling?"

"Good morning, Liya. I feel amazing!"

Aliyah frowned at her mother's extra perkiness. She wondered if the pain pills the doctor had prescribed were too strong. "I'm sorry I didn't call you last night. I got in late, and I didn't want to wake you. Do you need anything? I can stop by on my way to work—oh, your nurse, Erica, should come by this morning. I spoke with your doctor yesterday and set everything up."

"Aliyah, honey, I'm fine. You didn't have to do all that."

"Yes, I did! You had gallbladder surgery. I need to make sure someone is with you at all times. By the way, how is your pain?"

"A lot better. I slept through the night."

"That's great! What about food?"

Kaleen laughed. "I have a kitchen full of groceries you bought two days ago. Also, Rob bought food over last night. He's downstairs now, making us breakfast."

Rob was Kaleen's younger new boyfriend, whom Aliyah wasn't quite sold on.

"He spent the night?"

"Yeah, he did."

"Oh, cool."

Kaleen sighed.

"What?"

"You're not so good at hiding your distaste these days, Liya."

"What distaste? I like Rob."

"Sure, you do. Which is why you leave whenever he comes over?"

"Mom."

"It's true. I'm sure Rob has noticed, too."

Aliyah looked up at the ceiling. She hadn't

expected a heated discussion about her mother's love life that early in the morning.

"I miss David too, Liya. I wish he were still here, but he's not. Rob makes me happy. He's helping me to move on."

David was Kaleen's late boyfriend. He had passed away a year prior. The two had been together since Aliyah was thirteen. Although they were never married, David loved her mother very much, and vice versa. They hadn't needed a marriage certificate or rings to show their commitment.

When David died, he'd left a large lump sum of money to her mother. Because of that, she retired from her office job and traveled as she'd always desired.

"Have you decided what you want to do for your birthday next week?" Aliyah asked, determined to change the subject. It was too early in the morning for deep conversations.

"I have."

Aliyah released an inaudible sigh. "Where would you like to go?"

"Rob is taking me to Vegas."

Aliyah placed her stainless-steel coffee mug on the countertop. "That's pretty far, mom. Are you sure you should travel yet?"

"I spoke with Dr. Henderson. He said it won't be a problem."

Aliyah became annoyed. Even when David was alive, she and her mother spent their birthdays together. They would spend the entire day shopping and pampering themselves.

"Are you mad?"

"No," Aliyah lied. "Why would I be mad?"

"Since we usually spend the day together. It's my fault. I should have told Rob about our tradition."

"Don't worry about it. We can do something when you return. How long is your trip?"

"A week. We leave on Friday."

"I hope you have a good time, mom. You deserve to be happy."

"Thanks, sweetie."

Aliyah checked the time. "I better go. I have to finish getting ready for work. Love you, mom. I'll call you later."

"I Love you too, Liya."

After their call ended, Aliyah remained where she sat. She was far too old to pout, but that didn't stop her.

As she drove to work, Aliyah thought about her mother and how fast things transpired between her and Rob. The two had only been dating for six months. She wasn't jealous, but concerned. She'd heard of younger men taking advantage of older women, and she didn't want that to happen to her mother.

Inattentively, she reached down for her thermos to take a sip of her coffee and came up empty-handed. "Crap!" she yelled when she realized her thermos was at home on the kitchen counter.

She glanced at the clock; it read seven-thirty. Aliyah could have turned around, but she hated to start work after nine.

She pressed the Bluetooth button in her car. "Call Danita." After the third ring, Danita's voice came through the speakers.

"Aliyah?"

"Morning. Did I wake you, or have you left for work?"

"At seven-thirty? Why on earth would I head to work at this hour? Sorry, but you're the only one who arrives at work an hour before we open."

"Right," Aliyah agreed with a chuckle. "What time are you coming in?"

"Around nine. Why?"

"Can you stop by the coffee shop on forty-third street? I left my coffee home by mistake."

"Yeah, sure. I was going to stop by there to pick up a parfait. Do you want one?"

"No. Coffee will do."

"Okay."

"Thanks. You're a lifesaver."

"Don't mention it."

Aliyah ended their call. Her everything was back on course. Well, everything about that morning, that is: She still had to watch out for her mom and make sure she wasn't dating a gigolo. There was also the multi-million-dollar project she compromised by having sex with the client.

As the upcoming traffic light changed from yellow to red, Aliyah tapped on the brakes and slowed to a stop. After taking a deep breath, she let out a scream. "There, much better."

"Ma'am?"

At the sound of a voice, Aliyah turned her head. The female driver to her right rolled down her window and stared at her with concern.

"Yes?" Aliyah asked after she lowered her window.

"Are you all right?"

It took a moment to realize the woman was referring to her sudden outburst. "Oh, yes. It's been one of those mornings," she offered with a reassuring smile.

The woman nodded and returned the smile.

Sheepishly, Aliyah faced the front. When the light changed, she eased her foot off the brake and allowed the other car to pass. At the fear of involuntary seclusion, she made a mental note to work on her sporadic outbursts.

"Come on, Whitney. Help your girl out."

With the press of a button, *Whitney Houston's 'You Give Good Love'* played through the speakers and serenaded Aliyah to work.

"Good morning, Mr. Phillips. I hope I didn't keep you waiting long." Michael spoke as he entered the lobby of Mills and extended his hand.

"Good morning, and not at all. I just arrived myself."

"Great. What do you say we head toward my office?" Michael motioned for Ethan to follow him.

The men casually talked as they walked down the corridor. When they entered Michael's oversized office, Ethan sat across from him on the other side of his L-shaped mahogany wooden desk.

"Is there anything in particular you wanted to discuss other than a visit to the site? Is there an issue with the contract?"

"No, the contract is fine. I gave it to Ms. Carter last night—over dinner."

Emotions Ethan couldn't decipher flashed across Michael's face. At that observation, he made a mental note to dig more into Michael's relationship with

Aliyah.

"I see." Michael brought his hands together. "When do you want to visit the site?"

"This weekend, I would like for you and Ms. Carter to join me. We'll also tour Cherry Peak, its sister facility."

"You own Cherry Peak?"

Ethan nodded. "I do."

"What a coincidence. Last year, I took a ski trip up there with a few friends. That place looks amazing, by the way."

"Thanks. I inherited the lodge from my father, Henry Taylor. He and his late business partner, Albert Hensworth, built it back in 1970. We renovated it two years ago. Most of the structure is new."

"Wow! Henry Taylor is your father?"

Ethan smiled at the admiration in Michael's voice, but then his eyes saddened. "Yes, he was. He passed away almost two years ago."

"My condolences. Your father's reputation preceded him. I never worked directly with him, but I can tell you, his name carries a lot of weight around here. In fact, our firm designed the Chateau Hotel & Spa."

Ethan nodded. "Mills' reputation and history with my father were the reasons I considered your company for this project." *Aliyah Carter, the woman I plan to tie to my bed and fuck into submission*, sealed the deal. Ethan kept the last part to himself.

"I can assure you that you've made a wise choice. I speak for everyone when I say we're thrilled to be given such an opportunity. We have three project managers, but Aliyah is our chief project manager—frankly, the best. She's highly sought-after by our architects and contractors. She'll take care of you and make sure your vision comes to life."

Ethan pretended like his mind hadn't gone to a filthy place at the mention of Aliyah taking care of him. "I'm certain she will. I plan to keep her *very* busy. It would be best if she didn't work with other clients while assigned to me."

Once again, Michael displayed uneasiness, which led Ethan to conclude his relationship with Aliyah was more than professional.

"If you have no objections—regarding this weekend—I'll make necessary preparations for you and Ms. Carter's visit to Skykomish."

"I have none."

Ethan stood and extended his hand toward Michael.

With normality and ease, Michael accepted. "I'm looking forward to visiting the site and Cherry Peak."

"So am I. ... What time does Ms. Carter come in?" Ethan asked.

"Um..." Michael let go of Ethan's hand. "Actually, now."

His slight reluctance made Ethan smirk. If Michael and Aliyah were more than colleagues, he considered him a fool to let another man anywhere near her. "I'd like to wait for her. Can you show me to her office?"

"Sure, follow me."

Ethan didn't dislike Michael. From what he could tell, Michael was a decent guy. Still, he wanted him to know Aliyah belonged to him, and no other man had a chance.

When Aliyah arrived at Mills, for once, she and the receptionist weren't the only ones who'd come in early. Michael's silver Jaguar set parked in his space. He had never been an early bird. At his level, he didn't have to be. Neither did Aliyah, but that didn't stop her.

From the passenger's seat, Aliyah grabbed her black leather satchel and headed inside. She exchanged pleasantries with the security guard and then waved at the receptionist before walking toward the elevator. Once Inside, she pressed the button for the fifth floor. Out of habit, she checked her watch for the time. "Eight o'clock on the dot."

The elevator doors opened, and Aliyah made her way to her corner office. She was almost there when Michael appeared. He wore an expression Aliyah wasn't sure how to interpret.

"Good morning."

"Good … morning. What are you doing here so early?"

"I had a meeting with Mr. Phillips."

Aliyah's forehead creased. "A meeting?"

"He wanted to plan a visit to the site—are you sure the two of you had not met before yesterday?"

Aliyah ignored his question and reached inside her satchel to retrieve the contract. "Here."

Michael took the folder from her. He stepped closer and lowered his voice when he spoke again. "A couple of weeks ago, you made me come clean about a certain someone. Why do I feel you need to do the same?" Michael turned and headed in the opposite direction.

He was right. She'd invaded his privacy and pulled the friend card. Aliyah knew if she told Michael about Ethan, he wouldn't tell anyone. That was the least of her concerns. What did concern Aliyah was facing her feelings for Ethan. She never believed in love at first sight, and this damn sure wasn't the case. However, something was there. Something she wanted no parts of.

Aliyah stared in the direction Michael had walked. Now, she had two people she owed an apology. With a sigh, she continued toward her office. She reached for the key to unlock her door. As soon as the key slid into the keyhole, the hairs on the back of her neck stood.

Ethan's cologne.

With expectancy, she turned the knob and entered. There he sat on the other side of her desk, in her chair.

"Hello, Buttercup. Michael said you wouldn't keep me waiting long." Ethan linked his fingers and leaned back.

"Did he now?" If indeed Michael had used those exact words, Aliyah was certain he hadn't meant them the way Ethan suggested.

"Yes. He was the one who let me inside your office to wait for you. ... So, are you going to come in or not?"

Aliyah squinted at his arrogance. She closed the door and approached her desk. "What may I ask brings you here?"

"Business, unless there is something else you prefer, we discuss."

Aliyah's eyes remained fixed on Ethan. No matter

how sexy or painfully enticing he was, she wouldn't allow herself to be pulled into his thirst trap. "No, not at all, *Mr. Phillips.*"

"Business it is." He stood, stepped back, and offered her the chair.

As Aliyah maneuvered around the desk, she attempted to hide the unsettled nerves inside of her. The thought of her body being inches away from Ethan had her blood overheated.

She put her belongings on the desk, sat in her chair, and powered on her computer.

"These are for you." Ethan leaned over her shoulder and placed a set of rolled papers on the desk.

She closed her eyes briefly before she unrolled the papers. "What are these?"

"They're ski lodge blueprints."

"You've had them drawn up? You have an architect?"

"No. I wouldn't be here standing next to you if I did. These are the building plans for Cherry Peak."

Aliyah turned slightly in her chair. "You own that?"

"Yes, it belonged to my father. Have you ever been there?"

With preoccupation, Aliyah stared at the blueprints.

Ethan wrinkled his forehead. "What's the

matter?"

"Nothing." She shook her head. "I was thinking of my first and only visit there. I was eleven when my father took us—my mother and me. He taught me how to ski that winter." Aliyah left out the part about the vacation being the last one she and her parents went on as a family.

"Have you not gone skiing since?"

Still deep in thought, Aliyah looked up with hesitancy. "I have. My friends and I drove up to *Stevens Pass* last year." She scanned over the blueprints once more. "You're building a replica?"

"Larger and with changes, but yes. I brought these to give you an idea of what I have planned."

"As far as changes—"

"We'll go over those more in-depth when you visit the site this weekend."

"This weekend?"

Ethan's cell phone rang, and he turned away.

Aliyah took notice of how he glared at the screen with annoyance.

"I have to take this."

"Yeah."

He gave her another look, then answered his phone as he stepped out into the hall.

Aliyah couldn't be alone with Ethan. She didn't trust herself to be alone with him.

Chapter Three

"What in the hell do you want, Hillary?" Ethan growled into his phone. There was no use in trying to hide his aversion to her calling him.

"That's not a delightful way to speak to your wife."

"Soon to be ex-wife."

"Details," Hillary countered. As always, she seemed unbothered by his attitude.

"I don't have time for this shit. You have ten seconds, Hillary. You've already used up five."

"I want to sell you my shares," she blurted.

Quietness filled the line.

"Does that mean you're interested?" Hillary pressed.

Ethan wasn't sure of what game she played. Throughout their separation, Hillary waved her shares of the company owned jointly by their fathers in his face. She had often used them for leverage and hinted she would seek more if he went through with the divorce. Ethan had no problem with calling her bluff. His ownership of the other seventy-five percent of Taylor & Hensworth Investments was solid.

"There's a coffee shop on the corner of forty-third street. Meet me there in twenty minutes."

"You're here? In Seattle? I thought you weren't coming back until Thursday. Why didn't you tell me?"

"I just did." Ethan hit the end button, then dialed Todd. "I'll be out shortly."

"Yes, sir."

By the time Ethan made it to the elevator, his merry mood had disappeared. Bitterness and regret pumped through his veins. His divorce to Hillary was due to be finalized on Thursday, which was too far away for him.

Outside, Todd waited by the rear passenger door of the Escalade. Ethan entered and peered up toward Aliyah's office window.

"Where to, sir?" Todd asked once he settled behind the wheel.

"The coffee shop on the corner of forty-third."

"Yes, sir."

Ethan had chosen the location for two reasons: The closeness, and he knew it would repulse Hillary to sit and wait for him—especially there. She'd never stepped foot inside a place that didn't require reservations or valet parking. Aliyah probably enjoyed places like the coffee shop, Ethan assumed.

On cue, he reminisced about their brief meeting only minutes ago. He wondered why she wore such a worried look when he mentioned Cherry Peak. Ethan determined it was best if he didn't make a big deal of the situation at the time. Something told him the memory of her visit wasn't a pleasant one.

Like an addict, he inhaled his suit jacket. The scent of her perfume had transferred onto him.

Sweet.

Savory.

Intoxicating.

Her scent tempted him the minute she came within reach. Sure, in her office, he could have moved back and given her more space, but then Ethan wouldn't have earned the reward of the heavenly aroma he came to crave.

"I won't be long," Ethan told Todd as they pulled up to the curb of the coffee shop.

He exited the SUV and walked toward the entrance. He spotted Hillary sitting at a table; she looked pissed. A slow, satisfying grin crept onto

Ethan's face. Caught-up in Hillary's misery, he collided with a woman as he entered the coffee shop.

"Shit!" the woman shouted as the two cups of coffee and parfait she carried fell to the floor.

"My apologies. I should have been paying attention," Ethan said.

"Yes, you should have!—Oh, Mr. Phillips, it's you."

Ethan gave the pretty, petite, dark-skinned woman a once-over. "Do I know you?"

"I work for Mills Architectural & Designs—in marketing. Danita Jordan is my name."

"You'll have to forgive me once more. I don't recall meeting you."

"You didn't. I saw you walking around with Michael yesterday."

"I see." Ethan surveyed the mess on the floor. "We better clean this up before someone falls."

"I'll take care of it," Danita said.

"Are you sure?"

"Yes."

Ethan pulled a fifty-dollar bill from his wallet. "At least let me pay for your coffee and parfait."

"Fifty dollars is a little much; I only paid twelve."

"Humor me," Ethan said with a smile.

Danita chuckled and accepted the money from him. "Thanks."

"My apologies, again." Ethan placed a hand on

Danita's arm, then headed over to Hillary, who appeared even more irritated. "Hillary," he dryly greeted when he reached her table.

"Ethan."

"How much is this going to cost me?" he asked as he sat across from her.

"A million a share."

"You want me to give you twenty-five million dollars?"

Hillary rolled her eyes. "It's not like you don't have it. Twenty-five million will hardly put a dent in your bank account, Ethan."

"No, it won't. Nevertheless, I've already agreed to give you twenty-five million in our divorce settlement." Ethan detected desperation on her face. "Are you in some kind of trouble, Hillary?"

"No. It's just—my father left me with nothing but these stupid shares. I have bills and my upkeep to maintain."

Albert Hensworth, Hillary's father, had sold Ethan half of his Taylor & Hensworth shares before his passing. Upon his death, he'd willed the other twenty-five percent to Hillary, his only child. The rest of his hundred-million-dollar net worth—from other ventures—he'd donated to charity.

Albert was not only well-versed in matters of investments, but also his daughter. He knew she would squander away his money. The woman shelled out more cash than an ATM.

Ethan deduced Hillary knew the details of her father's will prior to his death. Hence, the reason she'd tricked him into marriage. As he sat in front of her, he regarded the designer clothes and diamonds she wore. Her current attire had to be worth fifty-thousand or more.

"He expected you to work for a living. Not exploit the fortune he sacrificed to build."

Hillary's eyes bugged.

Ethan knew how she hated to hear the truth, especially from him.

"Are you going to buy my shares or preach to me?"

"Xavier will draw up the paperwork and add them to the settlement. Twenty-five million and not a penny more." Ethan stood to leave.

"See you on Thursday," Hillary said triumphantly.

"Thursday."

Twenty-five million was nothing to Ethan. He would have paid more if it meant ridding himself of Hillary forever. There were few things Ethan regretted, and she sat at the top of that short-list. He would have never married her, if it hadn't been for their fathers friendship.

Hillary's shares were the only thing that tied them together. Anything he ever felt for her died when he learned how far she'd go for money.

"It's open." Aliyah glanced at the clock. Danita may have never been early, but she was never late. "What happened to you? Did you have to make the coffee?" Aliyah chuckled lightly.

"I had a brief run-in with Mr. Phillips."

Aliyah's body stiffened. "Ethan was at the coffee shop?"

When Danita lifted her brows, Aliyah knew the excitement in her voice had given her away. She couldn't continue with her charade much longer.

"Yeah. He met up with a pretty brunette. She acted high class, like she didn't belong there."

Aliyah thought of Ethan's phone call. "Must be his girlfriend."

"I don't think so. He didn't hug or kiss her. He appeared to wear a scowl when he sat across from her."

Why was she relieved? Aliyah changed the subject. "How much do I owe you?"

"Nothing. Mr. Phillips paid for it."

Of course, he did. "Listen, I need to apologize." Aliyah held up her hand. "Before you try to deny it, I should inform you that Michael told me about the two of you."

"What!" Danita set the cup holder with their coffee on Aliyah's desk.

"It's not his fault. I made him tell me."

"Why did you do that?"

"I'm sorry, I had no right." Aliyah pressed her hands together. "Please, accept my apology."

Danita stared at her. "I want the truth. What's the deal with you and Ethan?"

Aliyah broke eye contact. "I met him in Jamaica."

"When you went on vacation two months ago?"

"Yes. I spent my last night there with him."

"Are you serious? I mean, I figured you two knew each other, but not to that extent." Danita's brows knitted. "Did he know you worked here?"

Aliyah shook her head. "No, I don't think so. We slept together one time, and that's all."

Danita scoffed. "Aliyah, my dear. You don't sleep with a man like Ethan Phillips once."

Aliyah's eyes widened. "Trust me, you do."

"Was the sex that bad?"

"No. It was incredible; he scared the shit out of me."

"Then what's the problem?"

"A woman could lose herself in a man like Ethan. I can't afford to let that happen to me. I'm sure he prefers one-night stands, anyway."

"Then why is he here—at Mills?"

Aliyah shrugged. "He lives here. Mills is a notable architectural firm. Why wouldn't he choose us?"

"Is this all coincidental?"

"Yes, and he knows our relationship is strictly professional."

"You two have talked?"

"Yeah, last night. He gave me the contract to give to Michael."

Aliyah's phone rang. She looked down at the screen. "I need to take this. It's my mother."

"Sure."

"Hey." As Danita headed toward the door, Aliyah called out to her. "This stays between us. No one else here knows."

"No worries, my lips are sealed. I trust you'll do the same for me?"

Aliyah nodded, then answered her phone. "Hey, mom."

"Liya, honey, are you busy?"

"Not too busy for you. What's the matter?"

"Everything is fine with *me*."

"Then why do you sound so upset?"

"I just got off the phone with your father. He said he's been trying to contact you, but you won't take his calls. Is that true?"

Aliyah remained quiet. Two weeks ago, she had gotten a call from an unknown number. She didn't do unknown numbers, so she waited to see if they left a voicemail. They did. When Aliyah's estranged father's voice played back, anger swelled in her chest.

Why was he calling now? She didn't even listen to the entire voicemail before deleting it. Every call she received afterward, she ignored.

"Aliyah, are you there?"

"Yes, I'm here, and yes, it's true."

Kaleen sighed. "Sweetie, I think you should talk to your father."

"Why? He walked out of my life when I was twelve. After that, he sent birthday presents, Christmas gifts, and child support."

"He had a mini stroke."

Aliyah's heart skipped a beat. "When?"

"Two days ago, but he's back home now."

To ward off a headache, Aliyah squeezed the bridge of her nose.

"I know how bad it hurt you when he left, but he's reaching out to you. Today is all we have, Aliyah. Losing David taught me you shouldn't take time for granted. Tomorrow may never come."

Her mother's words rang true. Nonetheless, Aliyah wasn't ready to talk to her father. "I can't call him at this moment, but I promise I will."

"Thank you."

"Yeah, I better get back to work. I don't want to fall behind."

"Liya?"
"Yes."
"I love you."
"I love you too, mom."

It had been fifteen years—two months after her twelfth birthday—since Aliyah saw her father. The only thing she remembered was the anger he displayed that night. He wanted out of his marriage to her mother, and out from the house they shared.

Aliyah pressed her fingers against her temple as the sound of her father's raised voice, and her mother's sobs played in her head.

"I can't do this with you anymore. We're done!"
"What about Aliyah, Cornelius?"
"What about her?"
"You don't mean that!"
"Let go of me, Kaleen!"
Aliyah's mother's cries amplified as she begged Aliyah's father once more.
"Please, Cornelius. We can make this work!"
"We can't ... Stephanie is pregnant."
Kaleen inhaled sharply.
"I'm sorry you had to find out like this, but I'm done trying to make things work ... I'll send for the rest of my things. Goodbye, Kaleen."

Aliyah hated her father for walking out on them.

That night, after she cried herself to sleep, she vowed she'd never shed another tear for him. Nor did she want a relationship with him. Now, after all those years, her mother was forcing her to go back on her word.

As the day dwindled, Aliyah concluded that Michael was mad at her. She hadn't seen him since morning, and it was near six o'clock. That wasn't like him. He always found a reason to stop by her office.

They'd been friends since she started at Mills five years ago. His charismatic attitude, in addition to his hazel eyes, deep waves, and even deeper dimples, was irresistible. The words sexy and chocolate often slipped from the mouths of women, Aliyah knew.

Their friendship had been the subject of discussion in the past. Many people thought they were sleeping together. They found it hard to believe they worked so close without sex involved.

Although Michael was very handsome, he acted too much like a brother for Aliyah to feel anything sexual toward him. It had been the same for him. He'd often called her the nagging little sister he never wanted.

Aliyah packed up her things and decided she would stop by Michael's office on her way out.

She knocked on his door and waited for him to acknowledge her.

"Since when do you knock?" Michael asked, still

focused on the paperwork in front of him.

"Can I come in?"

"Since when do you ask for permission?"

Aliyah stepped forward. "You were right. I wasn't being honest about Ethan and me."

"I know."

Aliyah's forehead creased. "You do?"

"Danita told me."

"That heifer! She said she wouldn't tell anyone."

"You didn't think that included me? Seeing as you promised, you wouldn't tell anyone about us."

Aliyah twisted her mouth and nodded side to side. "Point taken, but technically I didn't. ... Does this mean you forgive me?"

Michael screwed up his face. "You haven't apologized!"

"I said I was sorry."

"No, you didn't."

"Well, I'm sorry. Don't make me beg."

Michael studied her. "All right, I forgive you." He returned his attention to the papers on his desk and stuffed them inside his briefcase. "You and Mr. Fancy-pants, huh?"

"Don't start." Aliyah narrowed her eyes and pointed a warning finger at him.

"My bad. ... One question."

Aliyah crossed her arms. "Yes?"

"How does it feel to get your groove back?"

"I mean it, Michael!" She picked up a pencil off his desk and threw it at him.

Michael held up his hands. "That was the last joke."

"It better be because nothing is going on between us."

"Which is why he's so adamant we visit the site this weekend?"

Aliyah's eyes widened. "You're coming too?"

"Yeah."

"Thank God!—I mean, that's good."

Michael chuckled and headed for the door.

"What? What's so funny?"

Michael lowered his voice. "You are, and the fact you think nothing is going on between you and Mr. Fancy-pants."

Aliyah gave him the evil eye.

"You want me to use his real name?"

"Right."

"As I was saying..." Michael pressed the button on the elevator. "The guy sat in my office this morning and staked his claim on you. We could have waited another week to tour the site, but I'm sure this is a ploy to spend time with you."

"Whatever, I'm the project manager. That's the only reason I'm coming along."

Michael eyed Aliyah with amusement. "If you were the janitor, he would still want you there."

As they stepped into the occupied elevator, Aliyah and Michael ceased their talk. All the while, the wheels in Aliyah's head spun.

When Aliyah made it to the restaurant, her three friends sat waiting. "Wow, Am I the last one to arrive?"

"Yep," Amanda confirmed as she ran a hand through her short, highlighted bob. AKA, her hairstyle for the week.

"Figures. Have you guys ordered?"

"Just drinks. We were waiting for you to order the rest," Tina said.

Aliyah noted Tina's nonchalant demeanor. Something was up with her. "Thanks." After taking a seat, she picked up the drink menu. Once she found a drink to her liking, she waved down a server. "Hi. Can I get a *White Russian*, please?"

"I'll have this right out."

"Thank you."

The other three women passed glances at one another.

"Rough day at work?" Serena asked.

"Something like that ... Ethan is here."

"What?" Amanda raised her perfectly arched brows.

"As in Montego Bay, Ethan?" Tina's chestnut eyes grew wide as she spoke.

"No, you mean as in the best sex of her life, Ethan," Amanda corrected.

Out of the three, Aliyah knew Amanda would be the one to give her the most crap. She took a deep breath and nodded.

All three women fired questions simultaneously.

Aliyah held up her hand. "Mills is designing his new ski resort. I'm the project manager. Nothing more."

"Did you tell him you worked there? That you lived here in Seattle?"

Aliyah smiled. The concern in Tina's voice matched the panic on her heart-shaped, honey-toned face. When she began to speak Spanish, Aliyah knew she had to calm her friend. "No, he lives here."

"Do you realize what this means?" Serena beamed with excitement and grabbed Aliyah's hand.

"What happened in Jamaica didn't stay in Jamaica," Amanda interjected.

Serena's piercing green eyes narrowed. She gave Amanda a look she'd often given her second-grade students. "That's not what I was going to say."

Aliyah placed her other hand on top of Serena's. "What were you going to say, hun?"

"That this is fate."

The smile on Aliyah's face disappeared. She removed her hand from Serena's and shook her head.

"Why not?"

The other two women knew where the conversation headed, and both tried to intervene.

"We should order now," Amanda suggested, hoping to defuse the bomb Serena had detonated.

"Yeah, I'm starving," Tina added.

As Aliyah reached for the menu, her phone chimed. She removed it from inside her purse, and read the message.

Ethan:
Pack your bags, Buttercup.
I'll see you this weekend.
Received: 6:30 PM.

All the background noises and voices faded away. *Was this fate? Was Serena right?* Aliyah didn't have the answer to that question. However, she knew what manifested in her stomach was more than butterflies.

Chapter Four

Downtown, Ethan sat behind his desk at Phillips Enterprise headquarters as he spoke to Xavier Willis, his lawyer and best friend.

"Hillary wants to sell them to you?"

"Yep. A million dollars a share."

Xavier shook his head. "What does Hillary need with all this money?"

"The hell if I know. She doesn't work, and I doubt she ever will. I'm sure she plans to live off it along with the other twenty-five million she's asking for in our settlement."

"We can fight the other twenty-five million. Hillary established her high-maintenance lifestyle long before she married you. As far as her abuse claim—"

"I just want this divorce over. The sooner, the better." Ethan had never laid a hand on Hillary, at least not how she claimed.

"Don't worry. I'll take care of everything. Hillary and her new boy-toy, Nixon, better not try to pull any crap tomorrow."

"They won't, or the deal is off. I told her, twenty-five million and not a penny more."

Ethan's desk phone rang. He recognized the Skykomish number that belonged to his cabin and hit the speaker button. "Good afternoon, Mrs. Hansen."

"Good afternoon, Mr. Phillips. I wanted to inform you that the rooms are ready for this weekend, sir."

"Did you place Ms. Carter in the suite next to me?"

"Yes, sir, I did."

"Thank you. What time is your grandson's play this evening?"

"Eight-thirty."

Ethan heard the excitement in her voice. He figured she thought he'd forgotten. "Take the rest of the day off and check your account. I put something extra in there for you to buy him a gift."

"Oh, my!"

"It's the least I could do."

"Thank you so much!" she said before disconnecting.

Xavier stared at Ethan.

"What?"

"Is there something you're not telling me?"

"Such as?"

"Such as, Ms. Carter. Who is she? I thought you said business associates from Mills were coming to the cabin for the weekend. You said nothing about entertaining a woman."

"I'm not." Ethan pretended to read over the papers in front of him.

"I call bullshit," Xavier said as he snatched the papers away.

Ethan leaned back in his chair and locked his hands behind his head. "Do you remember a couple of months ago when I was in Jamaica?"

"Yeah, what about it?"

"I met a woman. We spent her last night there together."

Xavier leaned forward. "Is this Ms. Carter that woman?"

Ethan nodded.

"Fantastic! You need to get back out there."

"It's not that simple."

Xavier tilted his head sideways. "What's the matter?" Concern showed on his face. "Don't tell me this is another Hillary situation."

"Hell, no!"

"Then what's with the look?"

"She wants nothing to do with me." Ethan shook his head as he spoke. "At least, not personally."

Xavier stared at him, mystified. "Am I missing something? If this woman wants nothing to do with you, why are you pursuing her?"

Ethan palmed his face. "Because I can't erase her from my damn system."

"As your lawyer, I have to advise you against stalking or forcing yourself on others. As your best friend, this is entertaining. The powerful Ethan Phillips, pining for a woman's attention."

Ethan threw the pen on his desk at Xavier. "I'm not pining after anyone!"

"When can I meet her?" Xavier asked with a chuckle.

"Saturday, when you visit the site."

"I can't wait to meet the special lady who has you all wound up."

"I'm not wound up," Ethan said through clenched teeth.

Xavier looked on with disbelief. "On another note … we're closing on the house next week."

"That was fast."

"Not really. We've been looking for six months. Kimberly has hired an interior decorator and a contractor. Hell, she's even started the guest list for our housewarming party—whenever that is. We haven't moved in yet, and she's driving me crazy."

Ethan laughed. "Sounds about right."

"I'm glad you find this humorous. Who knows, by

the time we have the housewarming party, you and Ms. Carter might be on the same page."

"Anything is possible," Ethan said with hopefulness.

On Thursday, Ethan sat across from Hillary and her lawyer; he hated the sight of them both. Ethan decided Nixon was far more suited for Hillary than he could have ever been. Not only was Nixon a slime-ball and a moron, but he was also a complete dick.

"Everything seems in order," Nixon said.

"Great!" Xavier replied. "Why don't you both do us *all* a favor and sign?"

"No need to get testy. I'm simply looking out for the best interest of my client. There were other offers to buy her shares. More lucrative offers, I should add." Nixon smirked and folded his fingers together.

Ethan's jaw clenched. He was seconds from withdrawing his offer. He glanced at Hillary—who'd been eye fucking him since he walked into the room—then back at Nixon. "What's the deal? Is your client selling or not?"

Hillary laid a hand on Nixon's shoulder and whispered something in his ear.

When Xavier kicked him underneath the table, Ethan knew he was telling him to be cool.

"Do we have a deal?" Xavier raised his brows and gestured with his hands.

This time Hillary answered.

"Yes." She smiled at Ethan and flipped her hair over her shoulder. "I know how much this company means to you."

Nixon's face fell. If Ethan had to guess, he would say Hillary had just screwed the poor schmuck. Ethan almost felt sorry for him. Almost.

Minutes later, Ethan was the sole owner of Taylor & Hensworth Investments. More importantly, he'd divorced Hillary.

"Pleasure doing business with you, gentlemen," Hillary said in an exaggerated sultry voice.

Ethan stood and headed for the door. He didn't care that he'd given away fifty million dollars. His freedom was worth every penny. With his mind focused on the weekend, he called his cabin to notify Mrs. Hansen he would head that way soon. He'd barely gotten down the hall when Hillary came running after him.

"Ethan, wait!"

"I'll be there soon, Mrs. Hansen." Ethan ended his

call and faced Hillary. "What now?" he asked, heeding her predatory smile.

"That was Mrs. Hansen? How is the old doll?"

"What do you want, Hillary?"

She bit her bottom lip, and Ethan wanted to vomit. Hillary may have been an attractive woman on the outside, but her insides were ugly to the core.

"You're staying at your cabin?"

"Yes."

Hillary reached out and touched Ethan's arm. Lustful hope filled her voice as she spoke. "Need some company? I thought perhaps you, and I could celebrate this special day together."

Ethan removed her hand, then looked back at her face. "Celebrate?"

"Yeah. Me, becoming fifty-million dollars richer. You, gaining full control of the company." Hillary trailed her fingers up and down Ethan's arm. "I did this for you. Nixon wasn't lying when he said there were other offers."

As Ethan shifted his body to leave, Hillary grabbed hold of his arm again. "You and I shared some amazing times, didn't we?" She bit her lower lip once more. "It wasn't always bad, was it?"

Ethan studied the woman that stood in front of him. No shame. Not an ounce of remorse for the shit she'd put him through that past year. "Sorry, Hillary, I'll pass. Besides, I already celebrated."

"When? With whom!"

Although he wasn't referring to the night he and Aliyah shared, images from that evening flashed through Ethan's mind. "I was talking about the day I stopped letting you sink your claws into me. The day I filed for divorce." As Hillary's confident expression turned into embarrassment, Ethan rejoiced on the inside.

"You and I were finished a long time ago, Hillary. Today, only made it official."

Ethan turned around and continued out the door. With Hillary gone, nothing stood between him and Aliyah. He could pursue her with a clear conscience.

Aliyah brought her bags downstairs and set them by the door. It was Friday, and her uneasiness about spending the weekend with Ethan had intensified. It had helped to know Michael would be there, but that sense of relief diminished as the week progressed.

Aliyah didn't believe that Ethan was a man who'd force himself on a woman. He wouldn't need to. It was her pride that kept her from admitting the truth; she yearned to be filled by him. Aliyah's issues with self-control didn't appear until after she met him.

Her mouth said one thing, but her body said something else.

At nine o'clock sharp, a black Chevy Tahoe pulled up in front of Aliyah's house. *This is it.* She grabbed her bags and headed out the front door. As she approached the SUV, a tall, bald, broad-shoulder, tan complexion man exited the driver's side. He wore a black suit and a pair of dark-tinted sunglasses. After opening the rear passenger's door, he walked to the back and opened the rear of the SUV before heading toward her.

"Hi, Ms. Carter. I'm Todd, Mr. Phillips's driver. I'll take those for you," he said as he reached for her bags.

"Thanks." Aliyah smiled and walked toward the door he'd opened for her. When two sets of eyes stared back at her, Aliyah bent over with laughter. Danita was sitting next to Michael, and the two looked quite comfortable.

"Why not, right?" she said. "The cat is out of the bag." Aliyah stepped inside and sat next to Michael.

"Yep, thanks to you," he replied.

Danita leaned forward. "You're not mad at me, are you?"

Aliyah squinted. "For what?"

"For telling Michael about you and Ethan."

"I had that coming." She turned to Michael.

"What's on the schedule for this weekend?"

"Ethan didn't tell you?"

"I didn't ask him. I asked you."

Michael returned her smugness as he spoke. "Per Mr. Phillips, we are going to tour Cherry Peak today. Tomorrow, we'll visit the site for Cedar Peak."

"Sounds great!" Aliyah pulled out her tablet and opened her reading app. She raised her hand to put her earpiece inside her ear, but Michael grabbed her arm.

"Do you plan on being antisocial this entire drive?"

Aliyah dropped her hands into her lap. "I'm not being antisocial. I figured I could use the time to catch up on my reading. Unless either of you has something interesting to talk about."

Michael opened his mouth.

"Except for my relationship—or lack thereof—with Ethan," Aliyah quickly added.

When Michael closed his mouth, she smirked and placed the earpieces in her ears.

They'd been driving for over an hour, and Aliyah had long ago lost interest in her reading material. Her eyes became glued to the tall trees surrounding the SUV as it drove down the winding road.

She glimpsed at Michael and Danita. They were holding hands, and Michael was caressing the top of

Danita's with his thumb.

Aliyah smiled. Even if love wasn't in the cards for her, she could still be happy for others. With that realization, she turned her attention back to the outside of the vehicle.

"We're here," Todd reported as he turned off the main road and onto a narrower road.

After a short drive, he pulled into the driveway of a two-story luxury log cabin. Its exterior consisted of a green metal roof, red cedar, and stone accents. It displayed large glass windows from every angle, most likely giving the cabin natural lighting during the day.

"This isn't a hotel," Aliyah said.

"No, this is Mr. Phillips's cabin," Todd informed.

Aliyah turned to Michael, silently asking if he knew about this. He shrugged and gaped back at the massive structure.

Once the SUV stopped in front of the three-car detached garage, they all stepped out.

The front door opened and captured everyone's attention. There Ethan stood, dressed in a fitted black sweater and a pair of dark denim jeans.

So, he's sexy as hell. Who cares? Aliyah wasn't sure if drool had formed, but as a precaution, she licked the corner of her mouth.

"Welcome," Ethan said as he walked over to greet them.

Aliyah briefly locked eyes with him, then moved toward the rear of the SUV, where Todd had unloaded their luggage.

"Ethan, this is Danita Jordan," Michael said. "She works in marketing. I hope you don't mind that I brought her along this weekend."

"No, not at all. My cabin has seven bedrooms. I'm sure we can accommodate, Ms. Jordan." Ethan looked at Danita. "Nice to see you again."

Danita blushed, and Michael struggled to hide his jealousy. "Again?" He searched Danita's face for an explanation.

Poor Michael, Aliyah thought.

Danita chuckled and laid a hand on Michael's arm. "I ran into Mr. Phillips—literally—the other day at the coffee shop."

Michael's shoulders relaxed, and that detail didn't go overlooked by Ethan. When Aliyah saw the subtle acknowledgment on his face, she knew he'd figured those two out.

"I believe I was the one who ran into you. Anyway, please, come in. Make yourselves at home." Ethan motioned for them to enter the cabin, then called for Aliyah.

At the sound of her name, Aliyah's head jerked up. "Yes."

"Todd and my housekeeper, Mrs. Hansen, will see to your bags. Please, come. I want to give you all a tour."

Aliyah set her suitcase on the ground and headed over to Ethan, waiting in the doorway. He grabbed her hand as she crossed the threshold and spoke loud enough for only her ears.

"You look exquisite."

Aliyah glanced at their connected hands and then at his face. "Thank you." Tactfully, she removed her hand from his and joined the others in the foyer.

They started on the first floor. Besides the standard rooms, Ethan showed them the billiards room, the home movie theater, and then the bowling alley.

Upstairs, he escorted them to their bedrooms. Aliyah observed he gave Danita a room close to Michael.

"You're next to me, Buttercup," he said after they dropped them off.

"Why am I not surprised?"

Ethan's eyes gleamed with enjoyment, but he didn't respond as he guided her to the other side.

"Here we are."

They stood in front of two mahogany wood, walnut-finished doors.

"This is my room?"

"Yes. Mine is a couple of doors down from you," he mentioned, while opening the set of doors.

Aliyah entered, and her mouth dropped. The room was anything but basic. Large masculine furniture may have filled the space, but the colors were romantic and cozy. "Oh, Ethan," she murmured as her eyes roamed over the Cortina King-size sleigh bed, made of the same wood as the bedroom doors.

"Yes."

She jumped from his proximity; unaware he'd walked into the room with her. "This is beautiful."

"Thank you. I wanted to make sure you had the best room in the cabin—well, my room is the best, but we're still working on that."

His words snapped her out of the trance. "We are?"

"Absolutely."

Aliyah narrowed her eyes. Ethan's complacency had her undecided on whether she should kiss him or throw him out of her room.

As though he read her mind, he stepped back. "I'll let you put your things away. Once you're done, come downstairs." With a wink, Ethan turned and walked out.

She stared at the closed door, then gave the room another look. "What have I gotten myself into?"

Chapter Five

*E*than left Aliyah's room and walked toward the staircase. As his foot hit the top step, he caught a glimpse of Michael and Danita tucked in the corner down the hall.

"Michael, we have to stop. Somebody might see us." Ethan heard Danita plead.

"I doubt anyone here would care."

"I do," Danita said, putting space between her and Michael.

Ethan hurried down the stairs. He reached the foyer and headed into the great room. Seconds later, Danita and Michael joined him.

"Did you settle in, okay?"

"Yes," they both said.

"Well, then." Ethan clasped his hands together. "Since you two are ready to go, you can head over to Cherry Peak. My assistant Kimberly is there waiting for you." Ethan ushered them toward the entrance and out the door. Outside, Todd stood waiting next to the Tahoe they had arrived by that morning.

"What about Aliyah?" Danita asked.

"Don't worry, Ms. Jordan. I'll bring her."

Once Danita was out of earshot, Michael spoke. "Good luck."

"Thanks," Ethan said, aware the man knew his game plan. He figured he should return the support. "Same to you."

The smirk on Michael's face faded and changed to discontent. He nodded, then turned and headed toward the SUV.

Ethan closed the door and walked back into the great room. The first part of his plan was going smoothly. He'd gotten Aliyah to himself. Now, all he had to do was wait.

It didn't take long before she made her appearance. As he admired the view, Ethan decided he'd never tire of watching her enter a room. He noted how she surveyed the area. "Are you looking for Danita and Michael?"

Aliyah turned her gaze back to him. "Yes, I was."

Not this time, Buttercup. It's just you and me. "They already headed over to the lodge." From across the room, Ethan noticed the flash of concern in her eyes. She tried to mask it, but it was too late. "We should do the same," he said as he stood and moved toward her.

"Sure."

Ethan kept his eyes on the road ahead. He thought about the drive he and Aliyah took to his mansion in Montego Bay. His agenda for that night was one thing: sex. That wasn't the case anymore. Aliyah Carter wasn't a woman who engaged in casual sex, at least not routinely.

That much, he was now sure of. So why did she sleep with him? Ethan figured he would hold on to that as if it somehow made him special. Still, he had work to do. It would take more than smooth talk to convince this woman to open up to him.

Sure, the attraction was there. The need and want pulsed through her veins as it did through his. Yet something kept her at bay.

"Are you from Seattle?" Ethan's voice filled the silence inside the car.

"No. I was born in Hawaii. My father met my mother there while serving in the military. I'm half Polynesian."

"So, you're a military brat, huh?"

Aliyah smiled. "Yes. We moved to Seattle when I was seven. My father retired from the military and started an electrical engineering company."

Ethan thought it over, then questioned her about Cherry Peak. "The other day, you seemed disappointed when you talked about your visit to Cherry Peak. Is there a reason for that, or did I imagine things?"

Aliyah glanced at him, and Ethan feared he'd asked the wrong question. "I didn't mean to be intrusive. If you don't want to answer, you don't have to."

"No, it's fine. That ski trip was our last family vacation. My mom and dad separated that year."

Ethan shifted his gaze between her and the road. "I'm sorry that happened to you and your parents. Hopefully, this trip will give you a better memory."

Aliyah shook her head. "Thanks, but that was fifteen years ago. It doesn't bother me anymore."

When she turned her head and stared out the window, he knew she was lying.

Once more, they drove in silence.

"What about you? Are you from Seattle?"

Ethan forced himself not to smile. She was conversing with him. Things were looking up. "Yes, I am."

"How did you become the renowned hotel mogul you are?"

"I took after my father, Henry Taylor. He and his friend Albert Hensworth became business partners back in the late sixties."

"Wait ... Taylor & Hensworth Investments? Mills designed a hotel for them. It was before my time, but they pride themselves on being a part of that structure's existence."

"They should," Ethan agreed. "That was one of the pioneer hotels built by Taylor & Hensworth."

Ethan wasn't sure, but she appeared more relaxed. He took the turn of events as a good sign and continued to talk. "After college, I worked for my father, then ten years ago, I ventured out on my own. Now, I have ten international hotels and forty in the US."

"Are these under Taylor & Hensworth?"

"No. Phillips Enterprise. However, both my father and his business partner passed away. Now, I'm the sole owner of their company." Ethan didn't deem the other details necessary.

Aliyah touched his shoulder. "I'm so sorry."

"Thank you."

They arrived at Cherry Peak, and Ethan circled the roundabout to the valet. After exiting the car, he came over to Aliyah's side. He studied her with intrigue as she took in everything.

"Is the lodge anything like you remember?"

Aliyah gave a half chuckle. "No, not at all. The place I remember was a lot smaller. Much cozier and quaint. This is ... over the top." She looked at Ethan. "I hope you don't take offense to me saying this, but I prefer the original version."

"Not at all."

The renovation hadn't been Ethan's idea. Hillary

had decided it needed a makeover. When Ethan saw how a sickly Albert reacted to his daughter showing interest in the business, he gave in. In any case, Ethan knew better. Every chance Hillary got to impress her friends and spend someone else's money, she took it.

Hillary's ideas didn't appeal to the seasoned guest. Like Aliyah, they preferred the homely and more inviting look. On a small but noticeable scale, reservations had suffered.

Ethan placed a hand on Aliyah's back. "Ready?"

"Yes."

Together, they walked through the sliding glass doors.

"Hello, Mr. Phillips ... Good morning, Mr. Phillips ... Hello, sir."

Ethan nodded at the people who spoke to him in passing, then shifted his attention back to Aliyah. He figured as she surveyed the lodge; she reflected on the childhood memory she'd shared with him.

When they reached the conference room, Danita and Michael sat engaged in a conversation with Kimberly.

"I hope we didn't keep you all waiting long," Aliyah said.

"Not at all. Hi, Ms. Carter. I'm Kimberly, Mr. Phillips's assistant. It's a pleasure to meet you."

Ethan gave his cousin a warning glare.

"Please, have a seat, and we'll begin," Kimberly said.

Suddenly, Ethan regretted he'd given her a job as his assistant. It also didn't help that she was married to Xavier. Ethan knew their conversation from earlier in the week had gotten back to her. That, in return, meant she would poke her nose around in his business. Ever since he split with Hillary, both had tried to set him up.

Ethan walked to the head of the table. He forced himself not to intervene when Kimberly sat beside Aliyah.

When the curvy strawberry-blonde with blue eyes approached them, Aliyah wasn't sure if she was friend or foe. Even with the large princess-cut diamond sitting on her wedding ring finger, Aliyah wasn't sure how to perceive Kimberly's relationship with Ethan. They were close, and that, strangely, irritated Aliyah.

However, as the meeting proceeded, Aliyah found herself affected by Kimberly's witty personality. There were also the sidebar discussions where Kimberly pitched Ethan to her. Almost like she was his wingman.

"Kimberly." Ethan's voice boomed with irritation. "Where is the second set of slides for Cedar Peak?"

"They're in there," she assured as she set her coffee mug down on the table.

"I don't see them."

"Hang on. I'm coming. Men," Kimberly muttered. "I swear, he would lose his head if it weren't attached to his body."

Aliyah laughed at the way the two behaved. She waited for Kimberly to return, then asked, "Are you and Ethan siblings?"

Kimberly shook her head. "No, but close enough. We're cousins."

"I knew it!" Aliyah said louder than intended.

"Care to share, ladies?" Ethan glared down at them.

Aliyah and Kimberly looked toward the front to find the others staring.

"No," Kimberly replied. "We were talking about something off-topic. It can wait."

Aliyah spotted the chastising gaze Ethan gave Kimberly.

"As I was saying ... Cedar Peak will be much like Cherry Peak's original structure, only larger with rooms. Guests will shop, eat, store gear, and sleep there. Cedar Peak will possess the cozy and quaint atmosphere certain people once enjoyed when they visited Cherry Peak."

Aliyah's heart fluttered as he repeated the words she'd used earlier.

"This will be a place where families reconnect and lovers rekindle their passion," he added.

Aliyah felt everyone's eyes on her and attempted to alter the subject. "I started the process. Based on the drawings you gave me, I narrowed down the list of architects and contractors I believe will carry out your vision. I will email them to you so that you can decide."

"That won't be necessary," Ethan said.

"Why not?"

"I'm going to let you choose the architect and contractor. After all, this is your vision, just as much as mine."

Aliyah opened and closed her mouth.

"That would be our food," Kimberly said before she walked over to answer the knocks at the conference room door.

"So, Ethan, do you come out here often?" Michael asked.

"No, not as much as I'd like to. Work keeps me busy. Although, I have arranged some time for us to enjoy the slopes after we tour the lodge today."

Aliyah stood to help Kimberly unload and set up the food. She needed to occupy her thoughts. As she listened to Ethan talk, she wanted to know more about him. On the drive there, she'd said too much about her personal life.

His inquisition about her childhood trip to Cherry Peak had taken her for a loop. It sounded like he cared.

Over the next hour, the group ate lunch and discussed the new resort. Afterward, they took a tour of Cherry Peak, changed into their ski gear, and headed over to the slopes.

Aliyah found the sight of the mountains and trees breathtaking.

"Who's up for a race?" Ethan asked.

Michael shook his head. "Not me."

"Count me out too. I'm not much of a skier," Danita chimed in.

"I'll race you," Aliyah said with pride. The way Ethan flashed his perfect white teeth made her skin flush. "How far?"

"All the way to the bottom," Ethan said. "You ready, Buttercup?"

His use of the endearment in public should have upset her. Around anyone other than Danita and Michael, it would have. Aliyah nodded and lowered her visor over her eyes. As she and Ethan got into the starting position, Michael counted them off.

"Three, two, one. Go!"

Like rockets, they launched off and zipped down

the slope. Pure adrenaline fueled Aliyah as she sliced through the wind. With her poles, she propelled herself farther. She bent slightly at the knees, leaned to the right, and then left.

Satisfied, she glanced over her shoulder. Her moves had put more distance between her and Ethan. In spite of this, Aliyah's victory became short-lived as she struggled to maintain her balance. After failing to prevent herself from falling, her body tumbled and rolled down the slope. Moments later, she came to a stop, but her head still spun.

"Aliyah!"

She heard Ethan's frantic call as he approached.

"Are you hurt!" Carefully, he removed her headgear.

"No. I must have turned my foot too far inward or something," she managed to say.

Ethan moved the dampened hair strands out of her face and inspected her.

"I'm all right," she tried to assure him.

"The hell you are!" He grabbed her face. "I thought, I thought you were ..."

His lips crashed down on hers. Aliyah told herself not to kiss him back, but she did, with just as much passion, if not more.

"Just say when." His words hummed against her forehead after he freed her lips.

"Ethan, I—"

"Aliyah!" Danita yelled.

"Is she okay!" Michael asked.

Both voices made Aliyah and Ethan look up.

"Yeah, I'm fine. I lost my footing."

"Come on, let's get you back to the lodge," Ethan told Aliyah as he helped her stand.

"We're coming too," Michael said.

"No. You guys don't have to do that. Stay here. I'll be back," Aliyah told them.

"Sorry, Buttercup, but after that fall, you're taking a break." Ethan pulled out his phone and dialed a number. "This is Ethan Phillips. I have a guest who needs medical attention. I'm bringing her in ... No, that won't be necessary. She's able to walk."

Aliyah started to protest, but her head throbbed. She allowed Ethan to lead her back up the mountain and over to the ski lift. Other than Ethan's questions of concern, they rode in silence. Neither spoke about the kiss, his words, or the ones Aliyah almost said.

When they entered the lobby, the nurse practitioner met them. "What happened?" the silver-haired woman asked.

"I lost my footing and tumbled down the slope." Aliyah felt Ethan squeeze her shoulder as she spoke.

"Half a mile," Ethan said with anger.

The woman's eyes widened. "Let's go into the office, so that I can examine you further. If you would, please, wait out here, Mr. Phillips. I'll need to see our guest in private," she said when Ethan attempted to go with them.

Aliyah looked back at Ethan; his features were unpleasant. "I'll be fine."

"Are you ready, Miss?"

Aliyah nodded and wished she hadn't. The movement made her head hurt more.

"I'll be right here," Ethan said.

After a head-to-toe assessment, two aspirins, and an hour of observation, the nurse practitioner allowed Aliyah to leave.

"Your neuro checks look good. I don't see signs of a concussion, but I advise you to take it easy for the rest of the day, and you shouldn't be alone," the nurse practitioner explained.

"I'm staying with friends."

"Good. As long as someone is with you at all times, I'll let you go."

"Thank you." Aliyah headed out the door. She went in search of Ethan. The way he'd fussed over her meant a lot, and she wanted to thank him.

Aliyah stepped out into the lobby and froze. She found Ethan, but it wasn't him who had caught her attention. The man with mocha skin standing next to him made her heart race.

"Wait, Sienna. Daddy is talking."

Aliyah's head turned in the direction of the

woman who had spoken. She gazed upon her swollen belly, and then the little girl two years older than the last and only time she saw her.

"Aliyah?"

Ethan's voice brought her back to him. When she looked his way, the chocolate eyes she'd once gazed into widened with recognition. Aliyah turned away and hurried to the restroom.

Calm down.

She stared at her reflection and exhaled through pursed lips, slowing her breaths. From the dispenser, she pulled out a paper towel, wet it, and dabbed it on her face. Several seconds passed, and she'd calmed herself enough to leave the restroom.

"Are you all right?" Ethan rushed toward Aliyah and grabbed her shoulders.

"Yes. I got a little light-headed."

Ethan loosened his grip. "What did the nurse practitioner say?"

"I don't have a concussion, but I should take it easy for the rest of the day. I think I should go back to the cabin."

"Sure, I'll drive you back and stay with you."

"No!"

Ethan clenched his jaw. "I'm not leaving you alone."

Aliyah placed her hand on his arm. "I won't be alone. Mrs. Hansen is there. Please, stay here. I'm all right. I just need to sit down and rest. Also, Michael and Danita will worry. They'll want to leave too."

Aliyah leaned forward and kissed Ethan's cheek; both the concern and hurt in his eyes compelled her to do so.

With a heavy sigh, Ethan dialed Todd. "I need you to take Ms. Carter back to the cabin. We're coming out now." Ethan ended the call and dialed the cabin. "Hi, Mrs. Hansen. Ms. Carter will return soon. She had a bad fall. Please, keep a close eye on her and see to her every need ... Thank you."

"Ethan. I'll be fine," Aliyah said when he ended the call.

She knew he wasn't pleased with her decision, but she needed some time alone. After seeing the man who broke her heart into a million pieces, Aliyah needed to put distance between herself and the man that had the power to do the same.

Chapter Six

As Todd drove away, Ethan figured he'd give them a ten to fifteen-minute head start before he followed. Aliyah was crazy if she thought he'd continue his day after witnessing her fall.

Once he located Michael and Danita, Ethan informed them he was heading to the cabin.

"We'll go back with you," Michael stated.

"Yeah." Danita agreed.

"She's going to be pissed," Ethan told them.

Michael shook his head. "She will have to be pissed. I'm not staying here while she's there with a concussion."

"The nurse practitioner ruled out a concussion."

"Oh, well, I would still rather go back with you," Michael said.

Ethan nodded. He, too, was still worried about Aliyah.

When they arrived back at the cabin, Danita and Michael went up to their rooms while Ethan searched for Mrs. Hansen. After speaking with her and checking in on Aliyah, he returned to the great room where Michael sat by himself.

"How is she?" Michael asked.

"She's asleep. Would you like a drink?"

"Sure, I could use one."

Ethan nodded. He knew that look. There was trouble in paradise. He handed Michael the glass of amber-colored liquid and sat. "How long have you known Aliyah?"

"Five years. It's safe to say she and I have crossed the line of mere colleagues."

His words made Ethan tense.

"Oh, no. Not like that. What I meant is she's the closest female friend I have. I'm the only man in her life who can say that. Heck, I'm the only man in her life—I mean—"

Ethan held up a hand. "I understand what you're trying to say."

Michael glanced at the fireplace. "I've never had to have this talk with a client, but I have to ask what your intentions are with her."

Ethan raised a brow. He could see Michael meant the question just as he interpreted.

"Aliyah is a grown woman, but she's also my friend who I care about."

Usually, Ethan wouldn't entertain such a question from a stranger. However, it was apparent Michael cared a lot for Aliyah. Ethan respected that. "I want to get to know her if she'll let me. I'll be honest, this is unfamiliar territory for me, but I'm invested in seeing where things lead."

"She's a tough one. You've got a fight on your hands," Michael warned.

"I figured as much. What about you?"

Michael shifted in the leather chair. "Same. This is new for me as well. Since she and I work together, things are complicated."

As Ethan drank his whiskey, he thought about the potential complications he and Aliyah faced. Hillary had been his only obstacle, and he'd taken care of her. In his mind, he replayed Aliyah's reaction to Lorenzo, an architect he'd hired in the past. Was he the reason Aliyah had her guard up?

Ethan stood. "I better start on dinner; I'm sure Aliyah will be hungry when she awakes."

Michael rubbed his stomach. " Need a hand? I'm getting hungry myself."

"Sure."

As they prepared dinner, Ethan contemplated asking Michael about Lorenzo. In the end, he determined it wouldn't be the best move. If Ethan questioned Michael about Aliyah's personal life, it would drive a bigger wedge between them. Only one person could give Ethan answers.

At nine o'clock, Aliyah awakened. She sat up and eyed the blanket that someone had placed over her.

Mrs. Hansen.

Aliyah made a mental note to thank her as she pushed back the covers and navigated through the dark room. Her hand reached for the bathroom's light and flipped the switch. In the mirror, she searched for signs of tears.

"You will never cry over another man."

With confidence, she straightened her posture, fixed her makeup, and headed downstairs to find the others.

As she entered the great room, laughter filled the space.

"Aliyah, you're up! How do you feel?" Danita asked. She had been the first to notice her.

"Better." Aliyah's eyes wandered over to Ethan.

"Are you hungry?" he asked.

"Yes."

Ethan stood and walked toward her. "Come, I'll fix you something."

Aliyah glanced at the others. "Are you guys coming too?"

"No, we already ate," Danita said. "I think I'm going to call it a night."

"Me too," Michael added.

Aliyah nodded and allowed Ethan to lead her to the other side of the house.

Inside the kitchen, he escorted her to the granite island, where she sat on one of the bar stools. She watched as he removed containers from the stainless-steel chef's refrigerator and made his way around the sizable kitchen. She observed how he moved with comfort and ease.

Minutes later, he set a plate of chicken and broccoli Alfredo in front of her.

"Dig-in."

Aliyah picked up her fork and took a bite. "Wow! Thank you. For the food and earlier today."

"My pleasure, Buttercup."

Aliyah lowered her head and shoved another forkful of Alfredo into her mouth. "Aren't you going to eat something, too?"

"I already ate, remember?"

"Right." Aliyah studied him as he sat across from her and played with the label on her water bottle. Something was on his mind. She thought about their kiss as she picked up her fork and swirled more pasta around it.

"Who is *he* to you?"

She could have pretended to be clueless, but that would have been otiose. Back at the lodge, she sensed Ethan knew the true reason for her reaction in the lobby. Aliyah paused and lowered her fork again. "Someone from my past. Someone I would like to forget," she explained, meeting his gaze.

Ethan nodded. "I can understand that."

"It's crazy how you go from loving a person to never wanting to see them again."

"I can't relate to the first part," Ethan confessed.

"You've never been in love?"

"No, I haven't."

Aliyah snickered. "You're one of the lucky ones. Don't worry. You're not missing out on anything. Love is a unicorn."

"A unicorn?"

"Yep, and so is a happy marriage."

"You don't believe in marriage?"

Aliyah shook her head.

"Are you serious?"

The horrid expression on Ethan's face made her laugh. "You do?"

"I do. With the right person, love and a happy marriage are possible."

"Interesting."

"Are you surprised?"

"Surprised, no. Confused, yes." Her forehead creased. "You say you believe in love and marriage, yet you're thirty year sold, and you've never experienced either?"

Ethan glanced at the counter. "I haven't found the right woman yet."

"Maybe you never will."

"I'd like to think differently. Is there a certain time frame when a person should get married?"

Aliyah shrugged. "No, there isn't."

They stared at each other in silence.

"Most marriages end in divorce sooner or later," Aliyah spoke again, carrying on with her case.

"Are you backing this up with statistical facts? Or is this your own belief?"

"My belief."

"Well, my parents would beg to differ," Ethan said.

"Mine wouldn't."

"Is that your final statement on the matter?"

"Yep," Aliyah said, before eating the last bite of pasta.

Ethan chuckled.

"What's so funny?"

"You are."

His reaction to her views on marriage was the same as others. The only difference was the disappointment he showed and the fact she cared. "What time is it?"

"Five minutes until ten."

Aliyah blew out a breath and rubbed the side of her neck.

"What's wrong? Are you in pain?"

She smiled at the worry on his face. "No, Bored. I shouldn't have taken a nap. I'm not sleepy."

Ethan displayed a wolfish grin. "Need something to occupy your time and tire you out?"

"Whatever."

"No, seriously." Ethan stood and pushed his bar stool forward. He walked over to her side and held out his hand. "Come on, Buttercup. I know what you need."

Aliyah squinted. "Where are we going?"

"You'll see." He guided her out of the kitchen and down to the billiards room. "How about a game of pool? Do you play?"

"I do, but…"

"But what?"

"I'm not certain this is a good idea. You're pretty competitive."

"Me! You're the one who almost suffered a concussion today."

Aliyah stifled a giggle as she moved farther into the room. "Perhaps a friendly game of pool won't hurt. There doesn't seem to be a risk involved."

Ethan headed over to the billiard rack. He removed two pool sticks and a chalk cube. "There's always a risk, Buttercup."

Aliyah joined him where he stood and took one of the sticks. "What's the risk? Better yet, the wager?"

"No wager. Just the truth."

"About what?" She held out her hand for the chalk he used to sharpen his stick.

"Us."

"That's easy. I don't need to beat you at a game of pool to answer your question," Aliyah said.

"Oh?"

"There is no us."

"There isn't?"

"Nope. I filed that night away as never to happen again."

"Ouch!" Ethan clutched his chest. "We might need some liquor to loosen you up a bit." He walked over to the bar. From inside the mini-fridge, he pulled out the ice tray and added two ice cubes to each glass. After he filled them both with bourbon, he headed back over to the pool table.

Aliyah accepted the glass he handed her. "Thank you."

"You're welcome."

They both took a sip from their glass and looked over the rim at one another.

With every second that passed, Aliyah's defenses

and armor lowered. Sure, she appeared in control, but she was losing herself.

"You might have filed our night away, but that wasn't the answer I was looking for," Ethan said.

"What answer are you looking for?"

"I want to know if you have thought about me since that night? Uh-uh." He shook his finger and stopped her from answering. "Not yet, Buttercup, after we play."

Aliyah raised her glass and took a sip. "Have it your way."

"I will." Ethan finished his drink and set the empty glass on a nearby table. "Since you're the guest of honor, I'll let you break."

Aliyah moved closer to the pool table. Her eyes remained fixed on Ethan as she positioned her stick in front of the balls. "Solid," she called out.

Over the next thirty minutes, they played back and forth. Each sunk two balls, then scratched. Finally, Ethan took the lead.

He focused on Aliyah as he called his last shot. "Eight ball, corner pocket."

The sound of the balls as they clashed echoed. Only this time, Ethan didn't make the shot. "Damn!" he said as he missed. "I lost."

Aliyah knew he could have made the shot; a twelve-year-old could have. "You lost on purpose, didn't you?"

Ethan raised his shoulders. "I might have."

"Why?"

As he walked in her direction, her pulse sped up.

"When you cum for me again—and trust me, Buttercup, you will—a game won't be the reason. It'll be because you can no longer deny what we both know. ... There *is* an 'us.'" Ethan closed the gap between them. "And every night, since that night, it's my face you see when you make yourself cum. It's my dick you wish would fill you. It's my hands you want on you, making your body come alive."

Aliyah sucked in a breath as the warmth of his teased her skin. She opened her mouth, but Ethan placed his finger on her lips.

"You can continue to delude yourself, but I was inside you. The sooner you come to terms with this, the better."

Aliyah closed her eyes as he removed his finger. She prepared herself for a kiss, but not for the words that came next.

"Now, if you'll excuse me. I'm going to bed; before I fuck you on this table and wake the whole damn house."

Ten minutes after Ethan had left, Aliyah still remained where she stood. Why did he have to be right? And why was admitting that so hard for her?

They couldn't go on like this. They needed to clear the air if they were going to work together.

Chapter Seven

*E*than hadn't intended for things to become so serious over a game of pool. His desire for Aliyah and her aloof demeanor were eating at him. Then there was Hillary.

He should have told Aliyah about his marriage. That night had presented him with the perfect opportunity to come clean. Then again, he would have lost any chance of a relationship with her, hence their chitchat in the kitchen.

Ethan got out of the shower. He dried off and stepped into a pair of pajama pants. As he walked toward the bed, knocks came at his door. Ethan knew it could only be one person.

He ran the towel through his hair and tossed it on the nearby chair. Another set of knocks came as he grabbed the knob.

Ethan swung the door open. As he expected, Aliyah stood on the other side. "Eyes up here,

Buttercup," he said when her gaze locked on his bare chest.

"We, we have to talk."

"I think we've done enough talking for tonight."

"No, we haven't. We need to talk about us."

"Us? The 'us' you claim doesn't exist?"

"Ethan, you're not being fair. You're a client—"

"You were my guest."

Aliyah sighed. "This is different."

"How?" Ethan inclined his head. "What's done is done. We both know your hesitation has nothing to do with me being a client."

When Aliyah shifted her weight and lowered her head, Ethan knew he was spot on. Too bad he didn't enjoy being right, at least not this time. She was vulnerable, which made him an asshole for putting her in that position. Ethan wanted Aliyah to come to him willingly. Not because he'd coerced her.

"You win, Buttercup." Ethan lifted Aliyah's chin. "I'll play nice. You want a business-only relationship, then that is all we'll be. Go get some sleep."

"I'm not sleepy, remember?"

Ethan sighed and leaned his head against the door. "You're killing me, Buttercup."

"Well, I'm not."

"In that case..." Ethan pulled Aliyah inside.

"What are you doing? Ethan, I'm not having sex with you!"

"Did I say you were?"

"No, I—"

"Come on." He pulled her toward his bed. When Aliyah pulled away again and crossed her arms, he figured he should explain his intentions. "You're going to talk, and I'm going to listen."

"Good, because—"

"Not about us."

Aliyah frowned. "Then what about?"

"Your plans for Cedar Peak." Ethan smiled. She hadn't expected him to say that.

"You want to talk about Cedar Peak?"

Ethan sat on the bed. "No, what I want is to strip you naked, tie you to my bed, and fuck you. Obviously, that will not happen ... tonight." He laid down, scooted over, and tucked his hands behind his head. "Come, Buttercup. Tell me your plans."

From what Ethan learned about Aliyah, he knew she wouldn't back down from a challenge. The bed gave, and she laid beside him. For a moment, they were silent. Ethan stared at the ceiling, and Aliyah, at him.

He changed positions, so he faced her. "Turn around."

"Why?"

"I want to hold you."

Aliyah turned around.

"Come closer."

She moved closer, and Ethan draped his arm over her waist.

"Ethan?"

"Yes."

"Are you hard!"

"As a fucking rock."

Aliyah squirmed in his arms.

"I wouldn't do that. It won't go down if you keep moving," Ethan cautioned as a chuckle escaped.

"I'm glad you're enjoying this."

"Sorry."

"I bet."

"What do you expect? I told you what I wanted. This is your fault."

"My fault?"

"Yep. Every time I think of you, this happens. Whenever you're near me, this happens."

Aliyah inhaled and shifted in his arms. The movement caused his dick to harden more.

"Shit!" Ethan groaned. "This isn't going to work." He grabbed a pillow and placed it in front of him. "Much better. Now, tell me your plans, Buttercup. I'm all ears."

It took a moment, but Aliyah talked. She started with the lobby and worked her way through the ski resort. At some point, her rambling made them both drift off to sleep.

Aliyah awakened in Ethan's bed the next morning, but he wasn't there. In his absence, she headed to her room to freshen up before she wandered downstairs to the kitchen.

"Good morning Ms. Carter. How do you feel?" Mrs. Hansen asked as she prepared Aliyah's coffee.

"Better."

"That's good. I was never much of a skier myself," Mrs. Hansen admitted.

Aliyah grabbed the back of her neck. "Actually, I'm not that bad. I go on a ski trip at least once a year with my friends. I got carried away yesterday. Ethan and I—I mean Mr. Phillips and I—were racing down the slopes, and I lost my footing."

Mrs. Hansen smiled and set a mug in front of Aliyah.

"Thanks." Aliyah wasn't sure how to perceive her kind expression. Was it one of pity or something else? Either way, she figured the woman was used to women fawning over her employer. "By the way, thank you for helping me yesterday."

"No need to thank me. You're one of the best patients I've ever cared for," Mrs. Hansen said.

"I must have dozed off while reading. When I

awakened, you had tucked me underneath the covers."

Mrs. Hansen blushed. "That wasn't me, dear."

"It wasn't?"

"No. Mr. Phillips came home shortly after you went up to your room. He must have tucked you in when he checked on you."

Aliyah lowered her eyes. Even after she'd told him not to worry, he came back. "Oh, I'll have to thank him when he comes down," she said, pretending she hadn't spent the night in his bed.

"I believe he already left. He ate breakfast about an hour ago and headed out."

Aliyah picked up the coffee mug and took a sip. After the words they exchanged and spending the night in Ethan's arms, Aliyah was nervous about seeing him. She'd been stewing over the situation all morning and still hadn't come closer to a decision.

She finished her coffee and waited downstairs for Danita and Michael.

"Where's Ethan?" Michael asked.

"I don't know. I haven't seen him this morning."

Michael nodded but looked at her unconvinced. "He must be at the site. We should head over."

As they walked out the door, Aliyah wondered about Michael. He seemed to know something she didn't. She ignored her paranoia and followed him along with Danita outside.

When they arrived at the site, Aliyah spotted Ethan's black Mercedes SUV. She tried but found the flash of electricity that jolted through her hard to ignore. Aliyah worried how much longer she could maintain her professional mannerism or unbothered facade.

"There he is, over there." Michael pointed in Ethan's direction, where he stood talking to a tall, well-built, light-skinned man.

"Hey, Ethan!" Michael called out and got his attention.

Ethan waved. "Be right there, Mike."

"Mike? Are you two bosom buddies now?"

Danita laughed at Aliyah's question, but quickly stopped when Michael glared at her.

Aliyah bit her inner cheek. With every step Ethan took, her legs turned to jelly.

Why must my body respond to this man? And why am I acting like a witch toward Michael?

"Morning, everyone. This is my attorney and best friend, Xavier Willis. Xavier, this is Michael Callaway, senior vice President of Mills architectural & Designs." As the two men shook hands, Ethan continued with the introductions. "This is Danita Jordan from marketing."

Danita gave Xavier a friendly smile.

"Last, and certainly not least, is Aliyah Carter, *my* project manager."

"Pleasure to meet you, Ms. Carter."

Xavier's lingered gaze was subtle, but Aliyah noticed. "Likewise, Mr. Willis."

"We were exploring," Ethan explained.

"Sounds fun. We'll join you," Michael said.

Together, the five of them examined the site while they discussed the development plans.

"What's going on with you?" Danita sat next to Aliyah as they waited for the others inside a small cafe in town.

Aliyah shifted in her seat. "Nothing."

"I doubt that. And since we only have a few minutes before the guys return, I think you should tell me now."

They'd become close. Not as close as Aliyah and her four best friends, but Aliyah trusted Danita. She scanned the cafe to ensure the three men weren't in sight—one in particular.

"Do you remember our conversation about Ethan and me?"

"Yes. You said it was a one-time thing."

"It was."

"Did something happen last night?"

"No, but I wanted it to." Aliyah pressed her hand against her forehead.

"What's so bad about wanting, Ethan? Give him a chance."

Aliyah made a quick negative movement with her head.

"How about this? You sleep with him one more time—to get him out of your system."

"I can't do that."

"Why not?"

"He's a client, and I don't have time to play some game only to be on the losing end."

"First off, if sleeping with him was going to jeopardize his contract with Mills, it would have done so. Second, I don't think he's playing a game. I think he really likes you."

"What makes you so sure?"

"I overheard Michael and Ethan talking."

Aliyah squinted. She knew something was up between them. "About me?"

"Yes, and me. They were discussing their women's problems. Michael asked Ethan what his intentions were with you."

Aliyah's eyes watered. She'd never had a brother or any male figure to take up for her. Over the years, Michael had become much more than her boss. He'd taken her under his wing and mentored her into the businesswoman she had become.

"What did he say?"

"He wants to see where things lead with the two

of you. ... If anything, you owe yourself this. I don't know all you've been through with men, but maybe he's the one."

Aliyah thought about her last three boyfriends. Kevin turned out to be gay. Eric was a porn addict with a sex doll obsession. Last was Lorenzo, the biggest trickster of them all. With her luck, Ethan was an alien from out of space.

"What about you and Michael? I know you don't like to talk about your relationship with him, but could he be the one?"

Danita smiled. "I hope so."

"Ladies."

Aliyah looked up at Ethan. As their eyes lingered, she asked herself if indeed he was the one. *It doesn't matter, Aliyah. It will never work.* She turned away and considered Danita's other option. One more time, and they could both walk away. The sexual tension between them would be resolved, and they'd go on without this pent-up frustration toward one another.

Aliyah's eyes roamed over Ethan as he sat on the opposite side of the table. *Yes, one last time would do it.*

This was his last night of torture, Ethan reminded himself as he stared at the moon from his bedroom window. With one arm propped against the wall, he raised the other with the glass of Hennessy to his lips. Ethan regretted his decision to have Aliyah stay in his cabin. Not only had it driven him to drink far more than usual, but it drove him crazy to sleep underneath the same roof and not touch her as he wanted.

When he held her in his arms the night before, it had been a miracle they hadn't slept together—more proof Ethan was falling hard for Aliyah. He never knew the true meaning of self-control until he met her.

Knock, knock.

"Who is it?"

"Me," the soft feminine voice answered.

Ethan set the glass on the stand, then walked over and opened the door.

His eyes wandered over Aliyah's short terrycloth robe, down to Aliyah's bare legs and feet. Either she was naked, or wore something that scantily covered her body. There was no way he could control himself if she lay in his bed tonight.

"How can I help you?"

"I wanted to talk to you ... about us." She bit her bottom lip.

"Not that again."

Aliyah glanced at the floor. "I guess I'm ready to admit otherwise."

"You guess?"

"You're not going to make this easy, are you?"

Ethan folded his arms as he considered how many times he had controlled himself in the last forty-eight hours.

"I'll admit you and I have an attraction toward one another, but the situation is delicate," Aliyah said.

"We've been through this."

"Yes, and like I told you, that was different, Ethan."

"Why are you standing at my door, Ms. Carter? What do you want?" When her eyes narrowed, he knew his use of formalities had affected her. "You have five seconds to tell me what you want."

"Five seconds! That's hardly enough time to have a meaningful conversation!"

"It's all the time I have. If you haven't spit it out by then, I'm pulling you inside this room, and I promise you, it won't be to talk or sleep."

"Ethan, I'm serious."

"So am I."

"Really? Five seconds?"

"One," Ethan counted.

In disbelief, Aliyah threw up her hands.

"Two."

"You're acting childish!"

"Three."

"Ethan, this is not—"

"Fuck it." He reached out and pulled her into his room. With his foot, Ethan kicked the door shut. When Aliyah tried to back away, he grabbed her robe and brought her closer. "I want you, Buttercup."

"I want you too, but—"

"Shh. No more talking. Unless it's my name or sounds of satisfaction coming from that pretty mouth of yours."

Ethan kissed her while his hand slid down and untied her robe. He reached inside her gown and exposed one of her warm, soft caramel breasts. His head bent and sucked her nipple before he grazed it with his teeth.

"Oh, Ethan!"

"Yes, just like that, Buttercup." He removed her robe, then picked her up and carried her to his bed.

"What's wrong?" Aliyah's voice shook as he hovered over her.

"You've tortured me for days."

"I didn't mean—"

Ethan kissed her. He slid his hand into her gown and removed her other breast. "I planned to go slow, but I want you so damn bad." He lowered his head and sucked her other nipple.

"Please!"

"What do you want, Buttercup?"

Aliyah met his tormented gaze. "Fuck me, Ethan. I want you to fuck me."

He released her breast and got out of bed.

"Where are you going?" Aliyah pushed herself up. She watched as Ethan removed the belt from her robe.

"Turn over."

Aliyah did as he instructed.

"Now, crawl toward the headboard."

She hesitated slightly, yet still complied.

Ethan knew Aliyah wasn't the submissive type. His chest swelled to know he was the only man who brought that side out of her. "Hold up your arms." He ordered as he walked over to the bed and climbed back inside.

Aliyah raised her arms and permitted Ethan to remove her nightgown.

A slow whistle of satisfaction blew through his lips. Fantasies of her body had often boggled him. She had forced him to live with only the memory of her.

"Lay on your stomach."

Once again, she obeyed.

After tying one end of the belt to the headboard, Ethan secured Aliyah's hands—with slack—to the other end of the belt. "Is it too tight?"

"No."

Back inside the bed, he squeezed her shoulders, then trailed his hands down her back, gently massaging the tissue underneath. Once he reached her ass, he palmed both cheeks and spread them apart. When she wiggled, Ethan took it as a sign she was nervous.

"Relax, Buttercup. We'll save that for another time—but only if you want." He spread her cheeks once more and licked her front to back, darting his tongue in and out of her sweet, wet canal.

"Please, Ethan!"

Ethan rubbed his body against hers. "You want this dick, Buttercup?"

"Yes!"

He laid on top of her and slid his full-length inside. "Damn, it feels so good to be home." He moved his hips and administered slow, deep strokes. "Tell me you didn't miss this."

Aliyah moaned. "I did."

"How do you want it?"

"Faster! Fuck me faster!"

Ethan gripped her hips and increased the speed.

"Yes, that feels so good!"

He loved that his woman wasn't afraid to tell him what she wanted. "What else do you want, Buttercup?"

"Harder, I want it harder!"

Ethan untied her hands. He pulled her up by the

waist onto her knees. He reached out, grabbed her hair, and plunged into her. "Like that?"

"Mmm-hmm."

"What was that?" He tightened his grip on her hair and slammed into her once more.

"Yes! Like that!"

"Do you want me to stop?"

"No, please, don't stop!"

Ethan let go of her hair and wrapped his hand around her neck. "Squeeze my dick with your pussy."

Aliyah used her muscles and did as he commanded.

"Do it again!"

She complied.

"Again!"

She complied once more.

Each time, he thrust deep inside her.

Slap!

His hand came down hard against her ass.

Slap!

"I'm about to cum!" Aliyah cried.

Ethan moved his hand from around her neck and pressed his thumb against her lips. "Suck."

Aliyah's warm mouth readily opened and engulfed his large thumb. Her muffled cries amplified as he viciously plowed into her.

"Are you ready!"

"Mmm!"

When he released inside her, Ethan felt his soul drain from his body. "Fuck!" He ran his hand down the glistening skin on her back, then tugged her into his arms as he collapsed.

"Ethan."

"Yes."

"We didn't use protection. I know we didn't last time, but—"

"I'm clean. I'll send you my physical in the morning, and you can see for yourself."

"I'm safe too ... but it's been two months since Jamaica and—"

"I would never hurt you or put you in harm's way, Buttercup. As far as Jamaica, there has been no one since you. If you must know, it had been six months before you."

Aliyah nodded.

"Any other concerns?" Ethan asked as he propped himself up on his elbow.

"No. I'm on birth control, so that takes care of that."

Ethan kissed her shoulder. "Go to sleep, Buttercup. I plan on fucking you in the morning."

Chapter Eight

Aliyah figured sneaking out of Ethan's room was a crappy thing to do. But she had no choice. As bad as she wanted Ethan, she couldn't allow that to happen. Danita's idea of sleeping with him one more time had blown up in Aliyah's face. Not only did she want more, but she felt herself going through withdrawals.

The fact he hadn't slept with anyone since their night in Jamaica stunned her. Was there more to their one night of passionate sex? Make those two nights, she thought as she sipped her coffee.

"Hey."

Aliyah jumped at the sound of Michael's voice. "Morning!" she said, trying to recover quickly.

"Why so jumpy?"

"I'm not jumpy."

"Right. Neither is a frog."

Aliyah ignored Michael's remark. "Are we still heading back to Seattle at eleven?"

"Yeah. Where's Ethan? I need to speak to him."

"How should I know? Why do you keep asking me?"

Michael's forehead creased. "You're the first person I've seen this morning. I thought maybe he'd been down to the kitchen."

"Uh-huh." Aliyah pursed her lips and narrowed her eyes.

"You know that I'm your boss, right?"

"Yes, Every day you insist on reminding me."

"Why do I put up with you?"

"Because I'm good at my job."

"No argument there," Michael said as he poured himself a cup of coffee and headed back out.

"Where are you going?" Aliyah asked before he disappeared.

"To find your boyfriend."

When Ethan awakened, it irritated him to discover an empty spot. Then the memory of Aliyah screaming his name while contracting on his cock invaded his thoughts. Any apprehension or doubt about her feelings toward him had diminished. She wanted him. She'd become addicted to the euphoric high only he gave her.

Aliyah was mistaken if she thought Ethan wouldn't give chase and simply give up. He was coming for her, but first, he wanted to make her sweat.

After he dressed, Ethan headed downstairs. On his way, he ran into Michael. They talked briefly about business and planned to meet later that week. When he and Michael reached the bottom of the stairs, they found Aliyah and Danita standing in the foyer with their luggage.

"Ladies," Ethan greeted.

"Good morning," they replied in unison.

"All packed and ready to go, I see. I hope you enjoyed your stay." Purposely, Ethan kept his eyes on Danita.

"I did. Thank you for your hospitality. I plan to revisit Cherry Peak soon."

"That's what I like to hear. Well, I won't hold you all any longer." Ethan patted Michael on the back and shook his hand. "We'll talk."

"Yes," Michael agreed.

Ethan finally looked at Aliyah. "Have a safe trip." He turned and walked off without waiting for her response.

Aliyah stared out the SUV's window as they drove back to Seattle. She knew sneaking out on Ethan was a cowardly move. Even so, Aliyah didn't do games, or did she? Hadn't she shown up at his door wearing nothing but her sheer nightgown and terry-cloth robe, ready to discuss her proposition?

Perhaps Ethan was the one who needed one more roll in the sack. Then, poof, he had no more use for her. If that were the case, Aliyah could live with that. She may have played the game, but she did not chase after men. If Ethan thought she would beg for his affection, he was mistaken.

"Hey, are you good?" Danita reached over and laid a hand on Aliyah's shoulder.

"Yeah, I'm fine."

Buzz, buzz.

Aliyah unlocked her phone and opened the email that came through. Three pages of Ethan's health record, including every STD and blood test known, stared back at her. The physical even showed his blood type.

"Humph, Mr. Perfect would be a type O."

"What's that?" Danita asked.

"Oh, nothing." Aliyah gave a fake smile and pulled her tablet from her shoulder bag. "I was thinking about the book I'm reading. Mr. Perfect."

*E*than didn't go out much; his schedule didn't permit him. When he made plans to meet with Michael, he wasn't sure he'd be able to keep them. Yet there they were, shooting pool and drinking beers.

"Damn, you're good at this!" Michael said as Ethan won another game.

"Don't tell Aliyah. Speaking of, how is she? Does she seem upset?"

"No, why do you ask? You two haven't been communicating?"

"No, not really. Throughout the week, we've messaged each other back and forth—about the project—but nothing else."

"Why do I get the notion you pissed her off?"

Ethan chuckled and picked up his pool stick. "I should have handled something differently."

"I see. Like I said, she's stubborn as a mule. Perhaps if you talk to her, you can work things out."

"You think?"

"There's a fifty-fifty chance," Michael said, before tossing back his beer.

"Maybe I should do a pop-up visit to see how the design process is coming along."

Michael laughed and held up a hand. "Hey, don't tell me. I don't need Aliyah thinking I had anything to do with this."

"Sure, you did." Ethan patted Michael on the shoulder. "It was your idea."

The smile on Michael's face vanished.

"I'm kidding. I promise to keep you out of it."

Ethan found Michael's seriousness laughable. His woman was a force to be reckoned with.

His woman.

On the way home, Ethan wondered if he could truly call Aliyah his. The way things were between them now wasn't any better than when he learned she lived in Seattle.

Ethan's phone buzzed. He glanced at the screen as he drove into his parking garage.

Hillary:
Hey there lover, are you back in town?
Received: 11:30 PM.

As he read the message, another came through.

Hillary:
My kitty cat has been a bad girl.
Why don't you come over and tame her?
Received: 11:31.

Ethan barely had time to press delete when his phone buzzed a third time. A picture of Hillary in nothing but a thong accompanied the last message.

Hillary:
I'll be waiting
Received: 11:32 PM.

Ethan cringed as though he heard Hillary's voice when he read the words. He didn't bother to respond. He blocked her number, something he thought he'd already done. Not that it mattered. If divorcing Hillary hadn't convinced her they were over, blocking her number wouldn't do much either.

*A*liyah reviewed the list of architects and contractors she had decided would be appropriate for Ethan's project. Along with Cherry Peak's original floor plans and the modifications they'd discussed over the weekend, she knew exactly how she wanted Cedar Peak to look.

Like they'd done over the last few days, Aliyah's thoughts drifted to Ethan. She still struggled to believe he'd left the design process up to her. She flipped through her planner. Four days had passed since she'd given her body to him once more.

They'd communicated, but only through text messages. Most messages regarded business, while a few consisted of the routine pleasantries.

'*How are you, Buttercup?*' Or '*How was your day, Buttercup?*' She'd left his last friendly "*Good morning, Buttercup,*" text on read and hadn't bothered to respond.

Professional, proficient, and business-minded were some words people had used to describe her. At that moment, Aliyah behaved less than any of those positive attributes.

Petty, prideful, and bitter were the words she leaned more toward; but she still got the job done. Mere proof that her passive aggressiveness hadn't affected her work ethic. She wouldn't let her and Ethan's personal relationship interfere with that.

Aliyah's phone rang. When she saw her mom's picture on the screen, her face lit up. That past week had been the longest since they'd gone without speaking.

"Hey, mom! How's your trip going?"

"It's been wonderful! I, I have something important I need to tell you."

Aliyah stopped typing and gave her undivided attention to her mother. "What is it?"

"I got married!"

"You did what!" Aliyah pushed her chair back from her desk and stood. "Mom! Are you serious!"

"I know what you're thinking, but it's not too soon."

"You barely know this guy!"

"Liya—"

"All I'm saying is that you should have gotten to know him better before—"

"Before what?"

Aliyah squeezed her eyes shut and shook her head. "I'm concerned."

"I appreciate your concern, but you don't need to be. Rob is a good guy."

Aliyah sighed.

"Honey, people are going to disappoint you; that's a part of life. You can't let that stop you from loving others."

"Mom—"

"No, listen. I worry about you."

"Why? I have a rewarding career, seven figures in the bank, and a perfect credit score on all three bureaus."

The sound Kaleen made told Aliyah the recap of

her portfolio did not impress her.

"That's not what I'm talking about. I worry about you finding love or, better yet, letting love find you."

Aliyah sat on the chaise by the window. Suddenly, dropping pennies down below didn't sound so bad.

"I'm worried you're so bitter about your father, Lorenzo, and those other guys; you won't let anyone inside your heart again."

"Mom, I'm not like you. I don't need to be loved." As soon as she finished her sentence, Aliyah regretted her words. She would never intentionally disrespect her mother.

"I married Rob because I want to be loved, and by the way, there's nothing wrong with wanting or needing love."

"You're right, there isn't'; and that's not what I meant." Aliyah knew from experience she wouldn't win this disagreement. "If you're happy, mom, I'm happy too."

"You mean that?"

"Yes, I do."

"When Rob and I come back on Monday, I want the three of us to go out for dinner."

"Sure." Aliyah sat back at her desk.

"Thank you, sweetie. This means a lot. I have to go, but I'll call you later. Love you—oh, and don't forget to call your dad. Because I know you haven't."

"Love you too. I won't forget." Aliyah hung up the

phone and covered her face. Her mother's second request that she call her father should have caused the irritation, but it was her important news that had Aliyah ready to scream. "Married!"

"You're getting married?" Michael asked as he walked in uninvited and sat across from her.

Aliyah uncovered her face and squinted. "Never. I was talking about my mom. She got married in Vegas over the weekend."

"To the new guy?"

"Yes."

"Wow! That was quick. You never mention they were so serious."

"I didn't know they were. I'm as baffled by this as you are." Aliyah's attention shifted toward the folder in Michael's hand. "What now? Something tells me I'm going to need headache medication soon."

Michael smiled and handed her the folder.

"When do you need this completed?" Aliyah inquired, while flipping through the documents.

"By the end of the day. They were due to accounting yesterday."

Aliyah huffed with annoyance. She was the queen of taking on more than she should. "Fine. Now, leave, so that I can save your butt."

"Actually"—Michael stood—"It's McCallister's butt. He was too chicken to ask you for help."

When Michael lingered, Aliyah figured there was

more to his visit. "Something else?"

"Have you spoken to Ethan?"

"Only through text." Aliyah lowered her gaze and began typing.

"We went out for drinks last night. You know, he's not a bad guy. I like him."

With more force than needed, Aliyah pressed the spacebar on the computer. "Oh, how lovely. You found a new friend to play with."

"You're mad at him, aren't you?"

Aliyah's fingers halted as she stared at Michael. She noticed the merriment displayed on his face. "Nope. Ethan Phillips is only a client to me."

"Sure, and Danita is just my friend."

He was trying to bait her, but Aliyah refused to talk about her and Ethan's relationship. "Out!" She pointed at the door.

Michael turned, then peeked over his shoulder. "Later, Buttercup."

Aliyah reached for her stapler, and Michael scurried away. She laughed because they both knew she wouldn't have thrown it at him.

♪*My milkshake brings all the boys to the yard*♪.

Aliyah pressed the button on the side of her phone to stop Tina's ringtone. Aliyah loved *Kelis*, but she hated that Tina had put that on her phone. Whenever she called while Aliyah was in public, people would stare.

"The next time I see you, I want you to take this mess off my phone."

"Are you busy? Can we meet somewhere?"

Tina's somber tone alarmed Aliyah. "Are you okay?"

"I need a rational mind."

"Now?" Aliyah looked over all the stuff she needed to finish.

"Yeah, I was hoping."

Aliyah thought about Tina's nonchalant attitude that past week at dinner. "Um, sure. Meet me at the coffee shop on forty-third street in thirty minutes."

"Thanks, Liya."

"I Got you ... Who knows, maybe you can be a sound mind for me too."

"Me?" Tina snorted. "I doubt that. You'd be better off calling a psychic hotline."

Aliyah laughed. "I'll see you in a bit."

Out of all of Aliyah's friends, Tina understood her the best. They could always tell when the other was going through something.

Twenty minutes later, Aliyah sat inside the coffee shop, waiting for Tina. As she sipped her coffee, a couple seated in the corner caught her attention. They were both attractive and seemed very much in love. Aliyah thought about the woman Danita said Ethan met up with there. Who was she to him?

Based on the description, she couldn't have been Kimberly.

♪*My milkshake brings all the boys to the yard*♪.

Tina's ringtone pulled Aliyah out of her trance. She looked up to find all eyes on her.

"Seriously?"

Tina wore a smirk as she held her phone to her ear.

"Do you see the dirty looks I get?"

"Maybe the ringtone isn't the cause."

"Here." Aliyah shoved her phone at Tina. "Take it off, now."

Tina wrinkled her nose and snatched the cell phone away from Aliyah. "You're no fun."

"So, I've been told." She waited until Tina sat. "What's this emergency meeting about?"

"Me, Ben, marriage."

Aliyah's eyes widened. "He proposed?"

"Yes," Tina said, handing Aliyah back her phone.

"What did you say?"

"I told him I wasn't ready."

"How did he take it?"

Tina blew out a breath as though she'd been holding it all morning. "Not well. He moved out."

"What!" Aliyah observed the tears that formed in Tina's eyes. "I'm so sorry, hun."

"Should I have said yes?" Tina shook her head. "Even if I'm not ready?"

"No. You did the right thing."

"I love him. I just don't want to marry him yet."

Aliyah gently rubbed Tina's back, attempting to soothe her friend. "Give him time. His pride is wounded right now."

"I don't know. I think he hates me," Tina sobbed.

"I doubt that." Aliyah reached for a napkin and handed it to Tina.

"What about you?" Tina sniffed back her tears. "What did you want to talk about?"

Before she answered, Aliyah took a long sip of her coffee. "Me and Ethan."

"Did something happen over the weekend?"

Aliyah nodded.

"You slept with him, didn't you?"

Aliyah nodded again.

"Was it good?"

Once more, she nodded. "This is awesome. It's like charades. I don't even have to talk," Aliyah said.

"Oh, yes, you do!" Tina lowered her voice. "I thought you said it was a one-time thing?"

"It should have been!" Aliyah covered her face. "I'm a hypocrite. I tell others what to do, but I can't control myself."

Tina removed Aliyah's hands from her face. "You're not a hypocrite. You're human and horny."

"Is it wrong that I miss him? That I want to see him again?"

"No, not at all."

"With him, it feels different. Like I could..."

"Fall in love again," Tina said, finishing Aliyah's sentence.

Aliyah closed her eyes.

"Go for it. See where things lead. Life is all about taking chances."

Aliyah laughed halfheartedly. "You sound like Danita."

"Who's Danita?"

"My friend who works in marketing. She and Michael—" Aliyah caught herself.

Tina raised a brow. "Michael is dating one of his employees?"

"I didn't say that."

"This is me you're talking to. I was your friend long before he was." Tina said through hooded eyes.

"Why must you do that?"

"What?"

"Put me in the middle. I hate that you guys dated. It makes things so awkward sometimes."

Tina rolled her eyes and folded her arms.

"You both are involved with other people. Who he dates shouldn't matter."

"So, he *is* dating her."

"Yes," Aliyah admitted. "She's nice. I like her a lot."

"Oh? Will she be joining the group?" Tina threw

back facetiously.

Not only did Aliyah regret her big mouth, but she also regretted that she had hooked Michael and Tina up. "Tina, it's been two years. You can't do this every time Michael dates someone. You broke up with him—for Ben!"

Tina remained silent.

"Listen, I love you to pieces. You know I do." Aliyah checked the time on her phone. "I have to go back; I have a ton of work to finish." She placed a tip on the table and scooted closer to Tina. "Stop pouting."

"I'm not pouting!"

"Yes, you are." Aliyah ignored Tina's irritated huff and continued. "Give Ben a couple of days. Then, invite him to dinner—make sure you're wearing one of your freak em dresses—and talk things out." Aliyah hugged Tina's neck and stood. "Call me later."

Tina finally caved and looked up at Aliyah. "One last thing before you go."

"Sure, what?"

"Is she prettier than me?"

Aliyah shook her head and threw up her hands. "I can't do this with you. Girl, bye."

"Is that a yes?" Tina shouted toward Aliyah's back, unbothered by the stares she received.

Chapter Nine

"I say we cut our losses. That place is a money pit."

"Yeah, I agree with Bryce," Edward said. "We've sunk a quarter of a million into this project."

Coolly, Ethan clicked his pen. Like his friends, Bryce Wells and Edward Duncan, he didn't like losing money or wasting time. However, he wasn't quite ready to walk away. Together, they had purchased a local nightclub; but neither knew the first thing about running it.

"I might know someone who can help," Ethan said, switching his gaze between the two men.

"Tell us," Bryce urged.

"Drew Watts."

"The owner of Stallions?" Bryce confirmed.

"Yes. He and I met a few years back. We kept in touch. If anyone knows how to make this work, he does."

"Yeah, but at what price?" Edward asked.

"Whatever he wants. Last year, his Stallions' nightclub chain brought in three-billion."

Bryce whistled.

"Do you think he'll be interested?" Edward asked.

"There's only one way to find out. I'll call him after we're done here."

"Oh, I think we are," Bryce said. Eager for Ethan to call Drew and rectify their situation.

Ethan gave both men a nod and signed off from their virtual meeting. As he unlocked his phone and searched for Drew's number, he wondered why Drew hadn't opened a Stallions in Seattle. The phone rang twice, and Drew picked up on the other end.

"Ethan, what's good?"

"You know me. Trying to make a living."

Drew chuckled. "From where I'm sitting, you're doing a great job of that."

"Same goes for you. In fact, I'm hoping you'll come on board with one of my newest projects."

Over the next thirty minutes, Ethan went over the details about the nightclub he and his friends had purchased. While they conversed, Drew told Ethan he'd planned to open a Stallions there in Seattle within the next year. However, with the possibility of becoming a partner in Ethan's nightclub investment, he would put those plans on hold. He agreed to a virtual meeting with the others that following week, to talk more in-depth.

Not only was Ethan glad Drew wanted in, but he was also glad he wouldn't have to compete with Stallions.

Satisfied with the progress of his day, he leaned back in his chair and scrolled through his text messages. Aliyah had read the last message he'd sent that morning, but hadn't bothered to respond.

Ethan knew he shouldn't have left things so vague between them at the cabin. It pissed him off that she had left his bed in the middle of the night, mainly because he had planned to do sinful things to her the next morning.

Perhaps he needed to see Michael's idea through and talk to her. "Time for a visit, Buttercup. I'm hungry."

"Where to, sir?" Todd asked once Ethan settled into the backseat of the Escalade.

"Mills Architectural & Designs."

"Copy that."

Four long nights had passed since Ethan tasted Aliyah and smelled her sweet, intoxicating fragrance. Michael wasn't lying when he said she was tough. That didn't matter to him. Ethan wasn't giving up on her.

No more games, Buttercup. Your time is up.

The second Todd parked in front of Mills, Ethan dialed Aliyah. To his surprise, his little prey answered.

"Are you avoiding me?"

"Why would I do that?"

The faint sound of sass in her voice aroused him. Ethan pictured her chin lifted in a challenge as she spoke. "Let's see... Every time I call, you're busy. When I text, you take hours to text back." He eyed the front of the car as Todd glanced in the rear-view mirror. Not wanting him to hear, Ethan opened the door and stepped out of the SUV.

"I have a lot of work to do. Between your project and my other clients, I stay swamped."

"I see." Ethan knew the 'other clients' part was a lie. Michael had informed him he'd only assigned Aliyah to his account. As Ethan took another step toward the entrance, he spotted Aliyah. "What about the way you left my bed?" Ethan asked as he moved out of her line of sight.

"We were only supposed to sleep together one last time," she said in a low tone.

Ethan heard the uncertainty in her voice. "Says who!" he demanded as he watched her press the button on the elevator.

"Me. If you had let me talk that night, you would know that. You're a client—"

"We've had this conversation, Buttercup. Since you insist on rehashing, we'll talk soon." Ethan hung up and waited for her to enter the elevator.

"*That* man is insatiable!" Aliyah shook her head and moved to the back.

She wanted to entertain the idea of more with Ethan, but she wasn't sure if she could handle the letdown when things blew up in her face. "It's better this way."

Aliyah laughed aloud. Someone was bound to think she was bat shit crazy for all the talking to herself she'd been doing.

Once the elevator reached her floor and the doors opened, she walked out.

"What the!—Ethan?" Aliyah clutched her chest as he dragged her into the stairwell. "Are you crazy! I just aged twenty years!"

"Yet, you're still beautiful as ever."

She suppressed a smile. "What do you want?"

"This." Ethan backed her up against the wall and smothered her lips with a kiss.

An involuntary weep eased from Aliyah's mouth as her body relaxed and betrayed her, as usual.

"Ethan! What are you doing?" she asked breathlessly, when his hand slid underneath her dress.

"Touching what's mine."

"Yours?" her voice came out shaky and unsure.

"Yes, all mine." He crushed his mouth against hers again. "These need to come off," he said, coming up for air.

"What?" Before she could protest, Aliyah felt her lace thong being torn on the side. Next, she felt Ethan's firm hand grip her ass. "We, we can't!"

"We can ... and we will," he mumbled into the crook of her neck.

"Please!" she pleaded when his teeth grazed her skin.

"I love when you beg." Ethan slid down her body and disappeared underneath her dress. "Spread your legs," his husky voice ordered before he opened her folds with his tongue.

"Oh!" Aliyah gripped one of his shoulders and threw her leg over the other. *No, no, no! What is wrong with me?* She Cursed herself for wanting this. For enjoying this. Her legs trembled when he latched onto her clit and continuously flicked the swollen nub.

"Always so sweet and juicy for me. Just the way I like it." Ethan plunged his tongue into her wetness and moved it around.

The sound of a door opening, followed by footsteps, made Aliyah look up toward the floor above them. "Ethan! We ... have to ... stop! Someone, someone is coming!"

"Yes, you are."

Aliyah covered her mouth and muffled her cries as her body bounced against the wall. Unable to stop herself, she grabbed the back of Ethan's head and pushed his face into her pussy. A whimper escaped her mouth just as the footsteps headed back up the stairs. "Ethan, please!" she cried out as he sucked her sensitive clit.

Ethan emerged from underneath her dress. He licked his lips and wiped the side of his mouth with her thong. "We're far from done. My place, tonight. Or you'll force me to take matters into my own hands again." Ethan stepped closer. He braced his hands against the wall, barricading her between them.

"Next time, I won't be so gentle." He pushed off the wall and headed down the stairwell.

Aliyah straightened her dress and fixed her hair to the best of her ability. As she reached for the knob, her phone buzzed.

Ethan:
1301 Spring St unit PH
Gate code:1343
Dinner will be ready at 8. Don't be late, Buttercup.

Received: 2:30 PM

At seven o'clock, Aliyah drove toward Ethan's penthouse. Several times she contemplated if she should retreat and make up an excuse. She knew once she entered his domain, there was no turning back. Over the last four days, she'd been delaying the inevitable. She was his. At least her body was. Perhaps if she didn't allow herself to fall too hard, she could hold on to what was left.

When she stepped off the elevator, she walked toward the only set of doors on the floor. She knocked and found the doors unlocked. She entered, and the smooth sounds of *The Isley Brothers 'Between the sheets'* played throughout the penthouse.

Aliyah closed the door and set her things on the Hepplewhite mahogany table. "Ethan?" she called out.

When he didn't answer, she walked farther into the penthouse. Abstract art hung on the wall. Various sculptures—of different materials—paired with modern furniture and neutral colors filled the open floor plan. Whoever Ethan hired, paid attention to every detail.

As Aliyah wandered through the large space, she found Ethan's bedroom. Her lace thong he'd ripped off of her, set in the center of his Cali-King bed. She retrieved it, then followed the faint sound of his voice.

She mischievously grinned as she stepped out of her shoes and tiptoed into the bathroom. Doing so rewarded her with a backside view of Ethan's body.

Aliyah walked farther inside until she stood by the shower door, then joined him as he harmonized with the song. The sound of her voice caused him to spin around.

"Right on time," he said with a smile.

"No, not really. I came for these." Aliyah held up her thong.

"Bullshit!" He opened the shower door and pulled her inside.

"Ethan! This is a two-hundred-dollar dress!"

"So, I'll buy you ten of them." He reached behind her and undid the zipper; the soaked fabric fell to the shower floor. His eyes roamed over her breasts, encased by her purple bra that matched the ripped thong in her hand. As he removed the netted material, Ethan locked eyes with her. "You look so delicious. I could devour you ... for days."

Beads of water dripped down Aliyah's face as she spoke. "Yeah, until you tire of me."

Ethan snatched the undergarments out of Aliyah's hand. His fast movement alarmed her.

"Hold out your arms," he ordered. When she hesitated, he gave her a reprimanding glare.

Aliyah did as he asked and allowed him to tie her hands together with her thong. He then positioned her arms over her head while his other slippery hand clasped the side of her neck.

Something wicked flashed in his eyes as he spoke. "I will never tire of you." Ethan leaned forward and lapped the bead of water from her bottom lip. "Is that understood, Buttercup?"

"Yes."

♪*I feel your love... surrounding me*♪.

Aliyah wasn't sure how, but the music in the background played louder.

Slowly, Ethan released her neck and slid his hand down to one of her breasts. "Do you know why I call you Buttercup?"

Caught up in the pleasure his fingers administered, she could only shake her head.

"These." Ethan ran his thumb back and forth over her breast as he lowered himself to take the hardened nipple inside his mouth.

"Ethan!" Aliyah's restrained hands dropped to the back of his neck. "Harder!" she demanded.

His lips unlatched her nipple and moved to her other breast. This time, he sucked harder.

As he traveled down her body and nibbled on her flesh, she came alive for him.

No longer could she deny the truth; she wanted this. Like in the stairwell, she propped her leg on his shoulder and relished in the sweet sensation of him eating her out.

Ethan slid his tongue deeper, and her tight inner walls squeezed it as she rode his face.

♫Oh, I like the way you receive me. Receive me, receive me♫.

Aliyah's entire body shook as her climax reached its peak. Every time she thought she'd experience the best orgasm of her life, he made her change her mind. She removed her leg from his shoulder and allowed him to stand.

Ethan lifted her tied arms back over his head, then hoisted her up, pushing her against the tiled wall. In one swift move, his thick, long shaft entered her.

Aliyah sucked in a breath and fisted his hair. With each thrust, she lost more control of herself.

Ethan leaned forward and pressed his forehead against hers. "No more running, Buttercup. This is how we should be. Do you understand?"

Aliyah nodded.

"No, I need to hear you say that shit."

Incoherently, she pressed her lips together.

"Say it!" Ethan delivered a deep thrust.

"Oh, fuck!"

"Say it!" he demanded as he repeated his actions.

"This ... this is how we should be!" she cried.

"No more what?"

"No more running!"

Ethan increased his speed. Sounds of pleasure filled the steamy bathroom as their flesh collided.

"You're mine, Buttercup." Unable to hold out any longer, he spilled into her warmth.

"All yours!" she confessed as her body succumbed to another intense orgasm.

Over dinner, Aliyah told Ethan about her mother's Vegas wedding that past weekend and her dinner plans with the newlyweds once they returned.

"What's the matter? You don't like him?"

Aliyah lifted her brows and shook her head. "I don't know him."

"Is that all?"

"He's younger than her?" Aliyah added, as she pushed her food around on the plate.

"How much younger?"

"Ten years."

"That's not so bad."

"Yeah, I guess not." Ethan's nonchalant tone didn't help to solidify Aliyah's woes about her mother and Rob. *Was she overreacting? Did she feel so jilted that she hated the thought of others acquiring love before her?*

"What are your plans for the weekend?"

Aliyah looked up from her plate. "Nothing, why?"

"I was thinking we'd... take a drive, have dinner, or catch a movie."

"Like a date?"

"Yeah, a date."

Aliyah smiled

"What's with the smile?"

"Nothing. I think it's cute that you want to take me on a date."

"Cute? People don't date anymore?"

"They do." Heat rushed to Aliyah's face.

"Then why are you so shocked that I want to take you on one?"

"No reason," she said, feeling foolish.

"What? Did you think this was only about sex?" Ethan gestured his hand between them.

Heat now consumed Aliyah's entire body. "No, that's not what I thought."

"I'm not just after what's between your legs. I want more, Buttercup."

Ethan's last words scared Aliyah; the sudden urge to run overwhelmed her. She cleared her throat, then spoke. "Have you ever been to Snohomish?"

"No, I haven't."

"They have a slew of antique shops. We could check them out—if you're up for it."

"I'm up for anything, Buttercup. In fact, we can make it a weekend trip. We'll leave tomorrow evening and come back on Sunday. How does that sound?"

"Perfect," she said, hoping her voice hadn't given away the uneasiness inside her. Falling for a man—

especially Ethan—was not in her plans.

Chapter Ten

After Aliyah left, Ethan prearranged for their stay in Snohomish. As he secured their room, he decided they would get to know each other over the weekend. He didn't like she thought their relationship was solely about sex.

Sure, for his entire adult life, Ethan had embarked on *sex-only* relationships, but not because he feared commitment. Over the years, casual sex was all he had time to entertain. Hillary had been the only woman he allowed things to go further with, and that was because she tricked him.

With Aliyah, he wanted something different. Something more permanent.

Ethan scrolled through the pictures displayed on his phone's screen. The B&B he'd chosen for them to stay at had been a cottage structure. He figured it would be the perfect place for Aliyah to open up and feel more comfortable with him.

Nice and slow. That's how Ethan wanted this to pan out. She's the one, he told himself.

Ethan's phone vibrated in his hand, and an unknown number appeared. He pressed decline, sending them to voicemail. Content with the reservation, he went to bed.

At 2 am, loud banging awakened Ethan. Sluggish and angry, he walked through the penthouse toward the front door.

"Hold your horses!" he bellowed out when the loud knocks came again. The minute he swung the door open, a drunken Hillary stumbled into his arms. "What the Fuck!"

"Why didn't you … answer … darling?" Hillary asked through slurred speech.

"You've got to be kidding me."

"We, we need to talk." She stood on her tiptoes and placed her face in front of his.

The loud odor of alcohol on her breath made his stomach turn. "No, no talking."

Ethan grabbed hold of Hillary's arm and led her to the kitchen. "Sit." He left her for a few seconds and brought back a glass of water. "Drink."

"Ethan—"

"I said no talking." He turned and headed out of the kitchen.

"Where are you going?" Hillary called after him.

"This is a fucking nightmare! It has to be!" Ethan picked up his phone off the nightstand. *"How did she get past the gate?"* He wondered as he called the security desk.

"Mr. Phillips, how can I help you, sir?"

"You can start by not allowing drunk women inside the building!"

"I'm, I'm sorry, sir. She told me she was your wife and showed me her driver's license. She was so out of it. I figured I should buzz her in."

Ethan palmed his face. He couldn't entirely blame the guard. "Next time, I don't care if the person tells you she's my mother and shows you a birth certificate. Call me first!"

"Yes, sir. I will."

Ethan's mother wouldn't have to ask for entry. She knew his code and also had an access key card.

"Shit!" Ethan slammed his phone down on the nightstand and walked over to his closet. When he returned to the kitchen, he wore a T-shirt and a pair of sweatpants. "Let's go, Hillary."

"What? Where?"

"I'm taking you home."

"I want to stay here with you," she slurred.

"Hell no!" Ethan tried to pull her up, but Hillary held on to the bar stool.

"Wait! I can't go home!"

Ethan's nostrils flared. "Why not?"

"Nixon is there." Hillary slumped her shoulders. "Boring ass Nixon."

"Not my problem." Once again, Ethan tried to pull her off the stool. This time, he was successful.

Hillary, a creature of habit, didn't pass up the opportunity to cop a feel.

Ethan quickly pushed her away. "The only reason I'm not sending your drunk ass home in a cab is because of your father!"

"He's dead." Hillary snorted. "He wouldn't give a shit. The bastard left me with nothing."

"Your father was an honorable man."

"Oh, that's right." Her voice took on an envious tone. "You're the *son* he always wanted. The *son* he wished he had instead of me—his ungrateful, useless daughter."

In the past, Ethan took pity on Hillary when she got like this. That was before she showed him her true colors. "Let's go!"

An hour and thirty minutes later, Ethan was back in his bed. Only he couldn't fall asleep. The last thing he needed was for Hillary to show up while Aliyah was there. As he'd done over the past few days, he thought of telling Aliyah about Hillary, then tossed the idea out. There was no way to do that without admitting everything.

With sleep hastily becoming a thing of the past, he hopped out of bed and headed to his home gym. Three miles on his treadmill would do the trick, he hoped.

Despite his unwanted visitor, Ethan felt energetic and ready for his weekend with Aliyah. He'd gotten five combined hours of sleep after his early morning workout.

"Morning, Cuz!"

"Cuz? What the heck has gotten into you?—never mind." Kimberly halted Ethan from answering her question. "I prefer not to hear about your roll in the sack with a supermodel posted somewhere on a billboard."

"Just give me my coffee and the stack of papers you're holding. I need to leave early today." Instead of waiting, Ethan grabbed both from Kimberly.

He observed the curiosity that flashed across her face.

"You never leave early."

"Yeah, well, I am today. Also, I'll be out of town this weekend." Ethan kept his eyes glued to the papers and hoped she wouldn't ask questions. However, he knew that was unlikely, especially when Kimberly pulled up a chair.

"Is this about Aliyah?"

Ethan glanced up from the contract he held. "It might be."

"I like her for you," Kimberly said approvingly.

"Between you and Xavier's enthusiasm for my love life, I'll be asking her to marry me by next fall."

"That's damn sure an upgrade. Hillary is a nasty piece of work."

Ethan snickered. "Don't remind me. I had the pleasure of driving her home at two-thirty this morning."

Kimberly furrowed her brows. "Why?"

"She showed up at my front door drunk. I'm glad Aliyah wasn't still there."

"You haven't told her about Hillary?"

"No—and don't give me that look. It's complicated."

"Try me." Kimberly folded her arms across her chest and stared at him with daggers.

"I was still married to Hillary when I met Aliyah."

"And?"

"If I tell Aliyah about Hillary, I'll have to tell her that part, too. I don't think it will go over well with her."

"Maybe it won't. Either way, the choice is hers," Kimberly reminded. "If you truly like her the way I believe you do. You need to be honest about everything ... What will happen if you and Aliyah run into Hillary? How do you think that's going to go?"

At the thought of Aliyah, not wanting anything to do with him, Ethan's mood plunged. He knew Kimberly was right, he just couldn't bring himself to tell Aliyah, not yet. "I'll talk to her."
"Good." Kimberly stood. "Where are you two going this weekend?"
"Snohomish, Antique shopping."
"Ooh! Next time, Xavier and I will have to tag along."
"Yeah." *If there is a next time.*

*I*t was like they'd stepped into another era. Historic homes, farms, and rows of locally owned shops in the downtown area had transported Aliyah back to yesteryear. Her original plan had been to explore the city of Snohomish with her mother. Somehow, she and Ethan were there together while her mother explored Vegas with her new husband.
Aliyah glanced over at the driver's seat.

"What?"

"Just looking."

"Like what you see?" Ethan licked his lips and waggled his brows.

"I'm still deciding," she said with a smile.

"What about the town?"

Aliyah glimpsed out the window. "Hmm? Let's see. It's small. There's not much traffic... I love it."

"Wait until you see where we are staying."

They pulled up to a quaint B&B that overlooked the river. A circular multi-colored stone paved driveway preceded the two-story white and green wooden structure. A small porch surrounded the entrance. Rose bushes trimmed the house while overgrown vines led to the second floor. From the red front door hung a 'Home Sweet Home' sign.

"What do you think?" Ethan asked.

"Perfection."

He nodded in agreement, unaware she had been referring to him. The word handsome hardly did Ethan justice, but she wouldn't tell him something he knew.

"Ready to go inside?"

"Yes!"

They exited the car, and Aliyah stood by as Ethan gathered their luggage from the trunk. "Will your car be safe here?" she questioned as they walked toward the entrance.

"I'll move it after we've checked in."

Aliyah walked forward. When they crossed the threshold and entered the foyer, she knew she would never forget her stay.

Romantic.

Charming.

Enchanting.

She sighed with wonder.

"Hi." Ethan addressed the woman behind the antique desk.

"Good afternoon, sir." The woman nodded at Aliyah. "Miss ... Would you be Mr. Phillips?" she asked, bringing her attention back to Ethan.

"Yes."

"Super! Your room is ready. My name is Kathy. I'm the owner."

"Nice to meet you, Kathy. You have a lovely place here." Aliyah complimented.

"Thank you, this cottage has been in my family for a long-time." Kathy viewed the luggage Ethan had brought in. "Is this all you have? If so, I'll show you to your room."

"Thanks." Ethan picked up both his and Aliyah's suitcase. "I left my car parked in the driveway," Ethan explained as they headed up the stairs.

"No need to worry, Mr. Phillips. You won't get towed out here."

After a quick climb to the second floor, they entered their room.

To the immediate right set a white loveseat, a cherry wood coffee table, and a modestly sized flat-screen mounted on the adjacent wall. A small kitchenette occupied the upper right corner of the room; Aliyah noted the coffee machine and mini-fridge tucked away. Straight ahead, a thick white duvet covered the black iron queen-size bed. Several gray and white pillows rested at the head, while a gray velvet throw laid across the bottom.

In the upper left corner, a set of French doors led to a balcony with an excellent view of the river. A big comfy white chair—perfect for reading—waited in front of the French doors. Aliyah noticed to the immediate left side of the room was another door and figured it to be the bathroom.

"I'll let you unpack." With a nod, Kathy left.

"This is amazing!" Aliyah walked over to the bed. "Do we have to leave?" The minute they stepped inside the romantic country-themed room, she hated they had only two nights to enjoy it.

"We can do whatever you want."

When he looked at her like that, Aliyah found deciding anything difficult. "What time is it?"

"A quarter till eight."

"Seems like we have time to do a little exploring. We should ask Kathy for some recommendations."

So far, so good, Ethan thought as he and Aliyah headed downstairs.

"What time do the restaurants usually close around here?" Ethan asked as they approached the desk.

"Ten. Except for Debbie's Diner, she stays open until midnight. If you're into simple foods like hamburgers and fries, she's got you covered. Anything fancier, you'll have to wait until tomorrow," Kathy said.

Ethan nodded. "I think we'll head over to Debbie's Diner."

"It's a five-minute drive from here. It sits right on the corner of Cider and Woods Creek Road. Tell her I sent you, and she'll give you a discount." Kathy looked Ethan over. "Not that you need one."

Amused by the woman's matter-of-fact behavior, Ethan glanced at Aliyah, who seemed amused as well.

"By the way...."

Ethan turned his head back in Kathy's direction. "Yes?"

"Here's a key to the front door." She came from

around the desk. "We have little nightlife around here. My guests rarely stay out late, so I seldom give out keys. With all things considered, I would rather you didn't wake me out of my slumber to let you in."

"Thank you. We don't plan to stay out too late," Ethan said.

"Good. Now that we have gotten that out of the way, I'm afraid I'll have to bid you both goodnight. I'm not a night owl like you young people. If there's a dire emergency, my room is down there by the kitchen." Kathy pointed in the direction. "If not, I'll see you both in the morning."

"Goodnight," Aliyah and Ethan said in unison, while concealing their smiles.

As Kathy instructed, they found the diner a short distance from the B&B.

"Welcome to Debbie's Diner. I'm Debbie; sit anywhere you like."

Aliyah and Ethan took a seat not too far from the door. Soon after, Debbie came over to their table.

"Visiting or passing through town?"

Ethan and Aliyah laughed.

"Sorry, most of the people that dine here are regulars. We recognize unfamiliar faces right away," Debbie explained.

"We're visiting," Aliyah said. "We plan on exploring the antique shops tomorrow."

"You came to the right place. Our antique shops have a mixture of old and new. Hopefully, you'll find something to your liking."

Aliyah smiled. "Thanks, I'm sure we will."

"If you don't mind me asking, where are you staying?"

"At Kathy's B&B up the road," Ethan told her.

"You are? She's my cousin. I wonder why she didn't tell me you two were coming?"

"I'm afraid I'm to blame," Ethan admitted. "She told me to let you know, but I forgot."

"Don't sweat it. Anyway, your meal is on the house."

"That's unnecessary," Ethan said.

"I know it is, but you're going to appease an old lady, aren't you?"

Ethan chuckled. "Well, since you twisted my arm."

Debbie patted him on the back. "Very good. Here are a couple of menus to look over."

"Actually, I'm not that hungry, Ms. Debbie," Aliyah said. "But I could go for something sweet, like pie."

"You're in luck; I took an apple pie out of the oven five minutes ago."

Ethan handed over his menu. "I'll take a slice of pie too — with a cup of coffee."

"What about you?" Debbie brought her attention

back to Aliyah. "Would you like a cup of coffee, too?"

"Yes, please."

"I'll have your slices of pies and coffees right out," Debbie assured, before heading back toward the counter.

"Feisty women must run in their family," Ethan said, referring to Kathy and Debbie.

"I think they're both cute."

"And I think you're beautiful."

"Thank you." Aliyah smiled and looked away.

Her bashful response to his compliment tugged at Ethan's heart. He decided he needed to know everything about this woman. "I notice you haven't mentioned siblings. Are you an only child?"

"Yes. What about you?"

Debbie returned with their order. She set a few packs of creamer and sugar on the table.

"Thank you, Debbie," Ethan said.

"No problem." She gave him a wink and walked away.

Ethan shook his head at the woman's playful advances.

"I think she likes you," Aliyah said.

"That's too bad, because I like you."

"I like you too, but you never answered my question."

Ethan smirked at Aliyah's change of the subject.

"Oh, yes, I have a younger brother. He lives in Paris."

"I've always wanted to go there."

"You should come with me in February. I travel there once a year. If I visit more often, Alex will swear I'm micromanaging?"

"Why is that?"

"He's the GM for my hotel there."

"Ah, I see. Having your family and friends working with you must be nice."

"It has its pros and cons. For instance, take my best friend Xavier and cousin Kim. They're married, so whenever they disagree, I get caught in the middle."

"Yeah, but having a sibling and others around has to be better than being the only child."

"Think of it this way. You never had to share your parents with anyone."

Aliyah shrugged. "If you say so."

The pain that appeared then disappeared quickly from her face, told Ethan she hadn't healed from childhood scars.

"Does your mom live in Seattle?" Aliyah asked.

"No. She lives in Palm Springs. After my father died, she sold their house and moved there."

"Why Palm Springs?"

"It's her hometown. Most of her family is there."

Aliyah nodded and ate another bite of her pie.

"Is this your mom's first marriage since your parents divorced?" Ethan asked, reverting the conversation to her.

"Yes, but it's not her first relationship. She dated a man named David for several years. He passed away a year ago. They were never married. That's why I can't understand her marrying Rob. I always thought she despised marriage as much as I do—if not more."

Ethan chose his next words carefully. "Why do you despise marriage?"

"I've never seen a positive representation of one. Men claim to love their wives, yet they cheat and have children outside of their marriage."

Ethan turned away.

"I'm sure all men are not cheaters. Just the ones I encounter—aside from you."

Aliyah's words made him look back at her. *Tell her now! No, disengage!* Before Ethan thought of a clever way to change the subject, Aliyah did.

"I've been meaning to ask you something, a favor."

"Anything." *Other than the truth.*

Aliyah looked around the diner. "I can't believe I'm going to ask you this. Feel free to say no."

"Buttercup, what is it?"

"Could you come to dinner with me on Monday?"

"With your mom and her husband?"

"Yeah. Usually, I wouldn't ask; but I think I might need a shock absorber."

"I'd love to."

The way she relaxed her shoulders, Ethan figured this had been difficult for her to ask. Aliyah Carter didn't like to depend on others.

With quietness and ease, they entered through the cottage's front door.

Ethan felt like a teen sneaking into his parent's home after staying out past curfew.

"Do you want to take your shower first?" He asked once they entered their room.

The twinkle in Aliyah's eyes told him things were about to get complicated.

"I figured we'd take one together."

Their eyes remained connected as Ethan nodded. He could do this. He could take a shower with her and keep his dick to himself. However, his hands were another story.

"This feels good," Aliyah said.

While she dipped her head underneath the water, Ethan leaned against the wall and admired the view. Flawless, he thought as his eyes wandered over every inch of her backside. He became jealous of the trickles of water that made their way down to her ample ass.

She peeked over her shoulder, and at once, their

night in Jamaica flashed in his mind. *"Show me how you make yourself cum."* His words echoed in his head.

"Ethan?"

He blinked and brought himself back to the present. "Yeah?" Aliyah faced him. The smirk she wore told him she'd been aware of his dirty thoughts.

"Will you wash me?"

Ethan took the washcloth from her outstretched hand and pulled her into his arms. Back and forth, he slid the cloth across her moistened skin. He reached for her ass and squeezed. When Aliyah moaned, he squeezed her ass again and backed her up against the wall.

With one hand, he clasped her wrists above her head. His mouth then explored the side of her neck where her pulse throbbed. Not to forget the original assignment, Ethan washed her breasts. He made circles around her nipples, causing them to harden under his touch.

Finally, he moved to her stomach, then lower to the place he called home.

A soft gasp slipped from her lips.

"You still with me, Buttercup?"

"Yes," she whimpered.

"Open your legs wider."

When she complied, he moved farther. Like an

oven, warmth engulfed his hand.

"Let me touch you."

Aliyah's soft voice made him pause.

"Please. I want to bathe you. It's only fair," she reasoned.

Ethan released his grip and allowed her to lower her arms. His eyes drifted down to his erection; precum dripped from the tip. His head snapped upward from her touch. In her hand, she held a washcloth. Ethan's eyes followed as she glided the soap-filled rag over his torso, down to his abdomen, and then his waist.

He groaned when she stroked and tightened her grip, letting her fingers slide back and forth over the tip of his dick. Barely able to withstand her touch, Ethan rested his forehead against the wall above her shoulder. "Fuck!"

"You still with me, babe?" Aliyah whispered in his ear.

Ethan reached down and grabbed her hand. "I think that area is clean enough."

"Are you sure?" she taunted.

"Yeah," his scruffy voice replied.

"How about your back?"

Ethan gave her one last glance, then turned around. The feel of Aliyah's hands gliding over his back sent an electrical current through him. With every touch, his urges became harder not to satisfy.

"There. All done," she said.

Ethan opened his eyes. As he moved forward, he pulled her underneath the shower head with him and together they rinsed the soap away.

Moments later—when they were dry, clothed, and in bed—Ethan wrapped his arms around Aliyah. He brought her near and kissed the back of her head. In such a short time, he felt more for her than he had for any other woman.

Chapter Eleven

As they explored the shops the next day, Aliyah and Ethan endured many stares. Despite their inability to blend in with the locals, they enjoyed themselves; the shop owners were actually welcoming and helpful.

"That's one of my favorites you're holding."

Aliyah smiled at the gray-haired woman who stepped from behind the small counter. She eyed her paint-stained smock, a tell-tell sign she not only sold but created the items in the shop. "It's become one of my favorites, too."

"Thank you. I made that one myself."

Aliyah rotated the rose-gold flower accented bowl in her hand. "The details are incredible!"

"It's a new design I've been working on."

"You have more pieces like this?"

"I do. They're home. I'm still working on them." The woman massaged her hands. "My arthritis doesn't allow me to work long hours anymore."

Aliyah knew the difficulties and pain in which the woman spoke. Her maternal grandmother suffered from severe arthritis until her passing. "Did you create all the items in your shop?"

"Not all. Some are from other locals. I try to help by selling their work."

"That's nice of you."

"It's how we survive around here. We stick together."

Aliyah nodded, then looked over in Ethan's direction. He talked to a man whom she presumed to be the woman's husband.

"Men are something, aren't they? They all bond over the same thing."

Aliyah regarded the antique truck in which Ethan, and the man discussed. "Yes, they do." She held up the bowl in her hands. "Much like us."

The woman chuckled. "How long?"

Aliyah squinted. "How long?"

"How long have you two been together?"

"We're sort of in the beginning stage."

"Oh? I would have guessed a year or two."

"Really? Why do you say that?"

"The way he looks at you. A man only looks at a woman like that when he has fallen in love."

Aliyah shifted uncomfortably. "I guess time will tell."

"Hey, what do you have there?" Ethan asked over Aliyah's shoulder.

"This is one of—I'm so sorry. Please forgive my manners. I didn't get your name."

"No need to apologize, dear. We were both yapping."

"As all women do," the gray-headed man added. His sea-blue eyes sparkled with delight.

"Oh, yeah? How about you quit yours while I'm talking?" Despite her scolding, the man kissed the woman's temple and zipped his mouth shut as he smiled at Aliyah.

"I'm Eve Sampson, and that"—she motioned her head backward—"is my husband, Grayson."

"It's nice to meet you both. I'm Aliyah, and this is Ethan."

"Her boyfriend," he added, shaking the woman's hand.

"This is one of Eve's designs. I'm going to buy it as a wedding present for my mom and Rob."

Ethan took the rose-gold bowl out of Aliyah's hand. "This is remarkable work, Mrs. Sampson."

"Thank you, young man."

Aliyah and Ethan followed Eve to the register.

"You said you have more. Is there any way I could see them?" Aliyah inquired.

"Sure. When are you leaving?"

"Tomorrow."

"I'm afraid I won't be finished by then. Do you have a card or some way I can contact you?"

"Yes." Aliyah pulled a business card out of her purse. "Here you go. Please call me. I would love to see them. Most likely purchase them all."

Eve smiled. "I'm happy to know my designs will find their way into the hands of someone who appreciates them ... Will this be all for you today?"

"Yes, I believe so."

They spent another three hours in various antique shops. At Glenda's Bakery, they gorged on several treats and skipped lunch. Finally, after another hour, they headed back to the B&B.

"Wow, I'm beat. Antique shopping is tiring." Aliyah kicked off her shoes and walked over to the bed.

"We can stay in," Ethan said. He set their bags inside the kitchenette, then joined her.

"Are you sure? I thought you wanted to check out that restaurant we passed on our way back."

"This is your trip, Buttercup. I want to do whatever you want to do."

"You're laying it on thick, aren't you?"

Ethan massaged Aliyah's shoulders. "Yep. Full-court press."

She may not have had brothers, but she'd watched enough basketball and knew what that meant.

"Hmm... in that case, why don't you see if they provide carry-out?"

Ethan kissed the side of her neck and stood.

Aliyah's eyes never left him as he pulled out his phone and searched for the restaurant online. Her mouth watered at the reminder of the last time they had sex. If she wasn't careful, she might find herself in Vegas like her mom.

Where in the hell did that come from?

"Found it."

"Great!" Aliyah forced a smile and pulled herself from her ridiculous thoughts.

"We're in luck with carry-out, but they're closing in an hour. Are you hungry now?"

"I am," she lied, to spare herself some alone time.

Ethan handed Aliyah his phone to look at the menu. It didn't take her long to decide what she wanted.

"I'm going to go with the beef, Stroganoff," she said as she handed Ethan back his phone.

"Sounds delicious. I think I'll copy you."

"Would it be all right if I stay here?"

"Sure." Ethan bent over and kissed her. "I'll be back."

Aliyah waited for him to leave. Then, like a virgin afraid to go all the way on prom night, she called Tina for help.

"Hey."

"Why do you sound like that?" Tina asked.

"Like what?"

"Anxious ... I thought you were going out of town with Ethan this weekend?"

"I did." Aliyah walked over to the French doors and stepped into the night air. "I'm standing on the balcony outside our room. It's gorgeous," she declared as she stared out at the river. With it being September, the harsh winter weather had yet to come.

"Then why are you talking to me and not lying in bed spread eagle?"

Aliyah scoffed. "I called to check on you—and we just got here yesterday evening."

"That's plenty of time to do the Hanky Panky."

Aliyah strolled back inside and sat on the sofa. She thought about the shower scene between her and Ethan that ended with them spooning in bed. "We took a shower together and slept in the same bed, but no, we didn't have sex. ... It was nice."

"Then what's the problem?"

"Who said there's a problem?"

"You did. You wouldn't have called me if there wasn't."

"Nothing is wrong. Ethan went to pick up our food, and I thought I'd check on you."

"Uh-huh."

Aliyah pressed her fingers to her forehead. "I'm

not good at this."

"No one is."

"The way we started—"

"Your relationship started as a one-night stand, so what? Worse things have happened. Like turning down your boyfriend of two years' marriage proposal."

"I'm sorry. I'm being dramatic over nothing, and you're dealing with that."

"Don't worry about it. Besides, I'm going to take your advice. I'll give Ben some time. If we're meant to be, we'll get through this."

Aliyah became amused by her ability to help others with their relationship, but not herself.

"Hey."

"Yeah," she said, almost certain of Tina's next words.

"Give him a chance."

"Right. Thanks for the talk."

"Anytime."

Aliyah put her phone down and took in the romantic, charm-filled room once more. How could one not want to stay in bed and cuddle all day? The thought of her and Ethan doing just that, put a smile on her face.

*H*e deserved a medal. Ethan's ability to keep his dick to himself had amazed him. The thought of Aliyah's soft body pressed against his—along with her scent and faint moans when she slept—had Ethan craving to be inside her. Maybe tonight, he would allow himself the privilege. *No, not this weekend.*

Ethan paid for their food and headed back to the B&B. He reached the room and found Aliyah sitting comfortably on the sofa in her oversize sweater. *Is that all she's wearing?* Ethan glanced toward the heavens. *Cut me some slack. I'm trying to do this right.*

"Hey, you're back." Aliyah stood and revealed her perfectly honey-toned legs.

"Yeah." He forced his eyes upward and unpacked their food. "Did you take a shower?"

"I did. I feel refreshed and starved."

Ethan nodded. "I hope you like Merlot. I grabbed us a bottle to go with dinner."

"Sounds good. Do you want to watch a movie while we eat?"

He eyeballed the sofa as he considered the invitation. If he sat next to Aliyah in such a small space, there was no way he wouldn't fuck her. He needed to handle the situation before he allowed himself to be so close.

"Sure. I'm going to take a quick shower first."

While I'm in there, I'll beat my meat, so I don't ram it into you.

"I'll set the food up."

With another nod, Ethan gathered his things and headed to the bathroom. Inside the shower, he muffled his throaty groans. The knowledge of Aliyah being only a few feet away caused him to have the most intense orgasm he'd ever experienced with his own hands.

After gaining control of his breaths, he washed, rinsed, and dried off. When he returned to the sitting area, he found Aliyah on the sofa with her legs crossed, engulfing Stroganoff.

Ethan sat beside her. "What are we watching?"

"I haven't picked anything yet."

"Let's see what we have." Ethan flipped through the channels. "The Notebook, Night of the Living Dead, Steel Mag—"

"Ooh! Night of the Living Dead. The original version? I love scary movies, especially the old-school slashers. You know, like *Halloween.*"

Ethan's eyes widened. "Who's your favorite? Jason, Freddy, or Michael Myers."

Aliyah scrunched up her face. "Michael Myers is the worst brother ever, and Freddy has the whole child murderer-molester thing going—so definitely not those two. I would have to say, Jason, the mama's boy."

"Wow, that was the most disturbingly accurate summation of those three characters."

Aliyah chuckled. "I've seen them all. I've watched the entire *Friday the 13th* franchise several times."

"If I ask you questions could you answer them?"

"Are you challenging my *Friday the 13th* IQ?"

"I am. That happens to be my favorite horror movie franchise, too."

With her game face intact, Aliyah turned sideways. "All right, Mr. Horror-Movie-Buff, bring it."

"I'll start with the easier questions."

Aliyah cocked an inviting brow.

"When did Jason start wearing the hockey mask?"

"That's easy. Part three. He got the mask after he killed Shelly in the barn."

Ethan nodded. "Impressive. You get bonus points for mentioning supporting characters." He turned, so he faced her. "Let's see if you know the answer to this one.... What year did Jason drown?"

Aliyah batted her eyes. "Fifty-seven."

"In part two, how long had it been since the murders from part one?"

"Five, long years," she said with a wink.

"Last one. ... How old was Tommy in part four?"

"Eight."

"Nope! He was twelve—and you claim to be a fan."

Aliyah laughed. "I got most of them right. Do I win anything?"

"Yeah, this." A soft peck had been all he planned to do, but like a magnetic force, she leaned into him and deepened their kiss. He couldn't help but take more.

As Ethan settled between her legs, his hands found their way underneath her. He didn't want to go back on his word, but damn, she felt good. Ethan found the willpower and pulled back. He would have been lying if he said the disappointment in her eyes wasn't a turn-on.

"That kiss makes me wonder what I would have won if I got the last question right."

Ethan's dick twitched. All he had to do was pull her panties to the side and show her. As much as he wanted to, he couldn't. He needed her to know this was more than sex. "We'll save the answer to that question for another time."

"Why?"

Ethan caressed the side of Aliyah's face. "I meant what I said. I want more, Buttercup."

"You want to date me."

"Yeah, I want to date you." He leaned in, and they kissed again. This time, his semi-hard erection stood at full attention and begged for release. "I should start the movie." He pushed himself up and located the TV remote.

The sound of Aliyah clearing her throat brought Ethan's eyes back in her direction. He followed her gaze to the tent inside his pants.

"Easy fix." He placed her legs in his lap. "You can't see it anymore."

Aliyah bit down on her bottom lip and swiped her foot back and forth. "True, but I can feel it."

Ethan groaned when she increased the pressure and stroked faster. "You're such a naughty girl."

"Yes, I am. What are you going to do about it?"

Was she challenging him? Did she not know she was agitating a bull? Ethan grabbed her foot. "I'm going to make you scream my name."

Aliyah's eyes widened.

"Not the way you think, Buttercup." Ethan tickled her foot and refused to let go.

"Okay! I'll stop! Ethan, please!" she pleaded.

"I still owe you," he forewarned after he released her foot.

"For what? You tickled me until I almost peed on myself."

Ethan belted out with laughter. "All right. A truce then."

"Truce," Aliyah agreed.

Chapter Twelve

On the way to the restaurant, Aliyah inwardly told herself to remain cool. Her mother was an adult. Although it bothered her, she knew little about Rob; Aliyah had to acknowledge her mother's happiness. That didn't mean she would not keep a watchful eye out.

Aliyah redirected her thoughts and shifted her gaze to the gorgeous man behind the wheel. At that moment, Ethan's eyes focused on the road. She smiled at how engrossed he seemed with the task.

She surprised herself when she invited him to come along. The more she dwelled on the matter, the more Aliyah realized she needed moral support to deal with her mother's new marital status.

With Ethan there, she wouldn't lose her composure and say the wrong thing. Aliyah rarely introduced someone she was dating to her mother so early, but lately, her life had been anything but normal.

"I should have mentioned this sooner, but my mom doesn't know I'm bringing a date. She's going to be shocked when she sees you."

"Are you setting me up, Buttercup? Is your mom going to give me the third degree?"

Aliyah rubbed her hand up and down Ethan's thigh. "Of course not," she said with a wink.

"Careful there. If you keep touching me like that, we won't make it to the restaurant."

Aliyah ceased her movement. *It's not too late to fall back. Stop this before things go too far, and he hurts you. Sure, you're all smiles now, but he's going to hurt you. They all do in the end.* Subconsciously, she sabotaged her and Ethan's new relationship.

"Hey, what's wrong?" Ethan asked.

"Nothing."

"Are you sure?"

"I'm fine. I promise to be on my best behavior—at the least, through dinner."

"That a girl." Ethan grabbed her hand and brought it to his lips.

Soon after, they reached the restaurant where Aliyah's mother and Rob awaited.

"Honey, who's this?" Kaleen's eyes fixated on Ethan as she hugged Aliyah.

"Mom, this is Ethan Phillips." Aliyah introduced

him as he held out his hand. "Ethan, this is my mother, Kaleen Carter."

"Um, that's Shaffer," Rob reminded.

"Right!" Aliyah squeezed her eyes shut. "Sorry, I forgot."

Rob offered her a smile and reached out his hand toward Ethan as he stood. "I'm Rob Shaffer Kaleen's husband."

"Aliyah has told me congratulations are in order," Ethan stated as he shook his hand.

"Yes. We got back from Vegas this morning."

As everyone took their seat, a server brought over a bottle of champagne. As he filled each glass, Kaleen's shocked expression remained intact.

"Ethan, you'll have to forgive me for staring, but my daughter neglected to tell me she was bringing someone with her. Are you two dating?"

"We met a couple of months ago while I was in Jamaica. More recently, Ethan hired Mills to build his new ski resort."

"You're a client?"

Ethan nodded and slid his hand over Aliyah's. "I am. In time, I hope to be much more to your daughter."

Aliyah locked eyes with Ethan. For a moment, she forgot about her mother and Rob.

"Well, I wish you both the best," Kaleen said, reminding Aliyah of her presence.

"To new beginnings," Rob added as he held up his glass for a toast.

Ethan and Aliyah did the same.

"To new beginnings," Kaleen repeated.

The four of them brought their glasses together and took a sip of the blush liquid.

"Before I forget..." Aliyah set the gift bag with the rose-gold bowl inside on the table. "I got this while in Snohomish."

"You went to Snohomish without me?"

"I've wanted to visit there for a while. You know that, mom."

An unspoken conversation occurred between Aliyah and her mother.

"Right." Kaleen rounded the table and hugged Aliyah as she accepted the gift.

The rest of the evening went by without incident. After Ethan and Kaleen excused themselves for a bathroom break, they left Aliyah alone with Rob.

"Aliyah, how have you been?"

"Good. How about you? Are you enjoying married life?"

"I am."

Aliyah drank from her glass. "Is this your first marriage?"

"No, it's not."

A previous marriage wasn't the end of the world,

but Aliyah wanted to know more. "How long were you married?"

"Eight years. She died of pneumonia."

"I'm sorry. I didn't—"

Rob held up a hand.

Aliyah felt awkward. She glanced toward the restrooms and wondered what kept her mother and Ethan.

"I know you don't approve of your mother marrying me, but I assure you I love her."

"It's not that I don't—" Aliyah paused. She looked away, then made eye contact with Rob once more. "You've only been dating for six months. That's hardly enough time. Sure, you may be fond of her, but love and marriage?"

Rob linked his hands. "When my late wife died, I realized a couple of things. One, life promised no one tomorrow, and two, time waits for no one."

Aliyah relaxed her shoulders and leaned back in her chair.

"Your mother and I have a connection that some couples don't achieve even after years of marriage. She's helped me to heal, and I'd like to think I have done the same for her."

Aliyah knew David's death had taken a toll on her mother. She had been there to witness the sleepless nights and pain she endured for several months. Once again, she thought of how happy her mother had been over the last six months. Rob had played a part in that.

Aliyah raised her glass and repeated the toast he'd made earlier. As she did so, relief crept onto Rob's face.

"Did we miss something?" Kaleen sat back in her seat next to Rob.

"No." Aliyah smiled and shook her head. "We were just talking. We both agreed on how important it is to spend time with the ones you love."

"Aww. Honey, that's so sweet."

As her mom kissed Rob, Aliyah decided to be more supportive. She would also give her relationship with Ethan a real chance.

"Is everything good?"

Aliyah laid her hand on top of Ethan's. "Absolutely."

I can do this. Aliyah repeated the words in her head as she paced her office. After dinner with her mother and Rob the previous night, she figured the time to face her father had come. She needed closure.

Aliyah walked over to the desk and picked up her phone. She searched for the number her father used to contact her. She located it under the three-week-old call log. "Here goes nothing." She pressed the call button and waited.

"Hello."

When a woman answered, Aliyah stalled.

His wife. Stephanie.

"Hello?"

Aliyah hung up. There was no way she could talk to the woman her father had chosen over her mother, whose child he'd chosen over her. No, things were better the way they were.

She threw her phone on the desk and sat in the chair behind it. When her phone rang, she pressed the off button. Her behavior may have been childish, but what she felt at the very moment was hate.

"What!" she yelled when someone knocked on her office door.

"I come in peace," Michael said defensively.

"Sorry," Aliyah apologized, but still wore a grimace.

"Whoa! What's with the angry face? Did things not go well with your mom last night?"

Aliyah's features softened. "It did. Ethan came with me."

"I see." Michael stuck his hands inside his pockets and rocked back on his heels. "So, you two have made up. I'm glad he took my advice."

"Your advice?"

"What I meant was … I told him to talk to you. To be open and honest about his feelings."

"Oh." Aliyah nodded. At the moment, she didn't have the mental capacity to dig deeper into Michael's new friendship with Ethan.

"If the evening went well, then what's with the mean mug?"

She didn't want to discuss that either, but Michael would only keep asking if she didn't tell him something. "I called my father."

Michael's eyes grew enormous. "When?"

"Before you knocked on the door."

"What did he say? Did you talk things out?—obviously, you didn't. You wouldn't be upset."

Aliyah's anger began to fade. The sight of Michael conversing with himself was comical. "I didn't talk to him. His wife answered."

"Did you talk to her?"

"No, I hung up!"

"You hung up?"

"I couldn't talk to that woman!" Aliyah raised her voice louder than intended.

A set of knocks at the door caught their attention. They both turned to see Danita standing at the entrance.

"Is everything okay?"

"Yes, everything is fine," Aliyah said.

"Oh, well, I'm on my way to the meeting. I figured

I would stop by to get you."

Michael looked at Aliyah, then back at Danita. "You go ahead. We'll be right there."

Once Danita left, Michael spoke again. "I didn't mean to upset you. From what you've told me about the situation, I can understand your hesitance to talk to your father and his wife."

Aliyah nodded. She hadn't intended to let her emotions get out of control. Michael wasn't to blame. "I'm sorry. I shouldn't have yelled at you."

"Apology accepted."

"We should head to the meeting. They won't start without us." Aliyah walked over to Michael. "After you, sir."

Michael chuckled and headed out the door.

As Aliyah followed, she knew the possibility of another attempt to reach her father was slim. He'd made his choice fifteen years ago. She'd gone this long without him in her life. She could go longer.

November~

*T*he great pretender he was, so he seemed. As Ethan prepped for his meeting at Mills, he thought about his newfound skill. Over the past two and a half months, when in the presence of Aliyah's colleagues, Ethan pretended he hadn't spent nights so deep inside her he'd taken up a permanent residency.

To Ethan, what others thought didn't matter. He knew Aliyah felt differently. She kept her personal life private. He did too, for the most part, except for her. He wanted the world to know she belonged to him. Yet still, he wouldn't force that upon her. He'd play the mere client role for as long as she needed him to.

At ten o'clock sharp, Ethan walked into Mills with one thing on his mind. His woman. He made his way to the elevator, and people greeted him as usual. Stuck on autopilot, Ethan responded and headed toward Aliyah's office. He arrived twenty minutes early for one reason: her.

He needed his fix. Something to pacify the beast inside until they were alone. Unfortunately, he wouldn't receive his dose. He approached Aliyah's opened office door and found her deep in conversation with a man.

Ethan cleared his throat and knocked. When Aliyah's head lifted, her hazel eyes gleamed with delight. In addition to the sexy red dress she wore, her reaction simmered the irritation inside of him.

"Mr. Phillips, please come in."

Her professional demeanor made Ethan once again become annoyed with the man responsible for their pretense.

"This is Cecil Rodriguez, the contractor who's going to build Cedar Peak. Timothy Reed is the architect. He'll be joining us soon."

She was all business and no play. Ethan understood, but that didn't stop his vexation. "I see. I came a little early to discuss something with you, but it can wait."

Aliyah's body language confirmed she'd interpreted the unsaid.

"After our meeting, I'm all yours."

Cecil coughed, and Ethan looked his way.

Unless he was drinking an imaginary beverage, Ethan concluded the man had seen through their act. He took a seat next to him, and they conversed about the resort.

Minutes later, Timothy joined them, followed by coffee and the bagels Aliyah had catered.

An hour into the meeting and Ethan checked out. Red—a blazing red, worn by the woman who stayed on his mind—is all he saw. Ethan took out his phone and sent her a text message.

Ethan:
How much longer, Buttercup.
Delivered: 11:30 AM.

Aliyah:
Not too much longer.
Do you have somewhere you need to be?
Received: 11:31 AM.

Ethan:
Yes, inside you.
11:32 AM.

Ethan looked up as he hit send. He wanted to see Aliyah's face when the message came through. When she bit down on her bottom lip, his dick swelled. If he weren't careful, Aliyah's colleagues would get one hell of a show.

He continued to watch her, waiting for her to dismiss the others. When she didn't, he took matters into his own hands.

"Gentlemen, it has been a pleasure. As you know, Ms. Carter has full control over the design and construction of Cedar Peak. If there are any issues, run them by her. If she feels I need to know, she will inform me."

Ethan winked at Aliyah—whose mouth hung ajar—then turned back to face the two men still sitting.

"Well." Cecil stood and extended his hand. "Mr.

Phillips, I can't wait to start." He glimpsed at Aliyah. "I'll be in touch." With that, he left.

One down, one cock blocker to go.

Ethan didn't wait for the other man to extend his hand. He beat him to the punch. "Thank you for your time, Timothy. Ms. Carter will be in touch."

Once the door closed and the coast was clear, Ethan walked toward Aliyah. She'd folded her hands across her chest, and wore a scowl that didn't match her sexy red dress.

"Am I in trouble?" Ethan asked. He stuck his hands inside his pockets and tilted his head sideways.

"You could have waited for me to end the meeting."

"You're right. I'm sorry. Will you forgive me?" He moved closer, knowing she wouldn't refuse him.

"Yes."

Ethan cupped the side of her face while his other hand gripped her hip. "Now, can I please have my fix?" he begged, then took the kiss he wanted. "Mmm. Jane, make *Tarzan* better."

Aliyah's vibrant laugh shook her whole body, causing him to laugh too.

"I can't stay mad at you, but I do have to get back to work," she told him.

"I'll leave in one condition."

"I'm listening."

"You, me, dinner tonight."

"Jane accepts your invitation."

Ethan kissed her forehead. "Until tonight." He ran his hands over her hips. "Make sure you're still wearing this dress. I want to be the one that takes it off you," he said, then headed toward the door.

Chapter Thirteen

*A*liyah wasn't an addict. She could quit Ethan anytime she wanted. Not that she wanted to. Things were good.
Really good.
Too good.
Don't do this, Liya. Leave doubt where it belongs, buried.

She grabbed her purse and stepped out of her car. She pressed the alarm and headed to Ethan's parking garage elevator. Every time Aliyah came to his penthouse, it felt like the first time.

To say the sex was good would say nothing at all. *There's more here. No, it's too early. Too soon.*

Aliyah knocked on Ethan's door and waited for her obsession to answer.

The door opened, and he pulled her inside. Their lips touched, their tongues danced, and their hands explored. Who needed words to say hello when your body did a better job?

"I have something for you!" Ethan said.

"What is it?"

"A collection."

"A collection of what?"

"You're supposed to guess."

"Um..." She screwed up her face. "I got nothing."

Ethan grabbed Aliyah's hand and guided her to the kitchen. He retrieved the gift bag from the counter and held it out.

"Ooh! Aliyah's eyes lit up." She reached for the bag, but Ethan yanked it back. "You dirty little tease."

"All right. I'll play nice." Ethan handed her the bag.

"Where did you find these?" she asked as she pulled the entire *Friday the 13th* collection from inside.

"Online. There are a couple of DVDs with exclusive footage in there, too."

Aliyah wrapped her arms around Ethan's neck. "Thank you! I appreciate this."

"Mmm-hmm. I did it for me, too."

"Oh?"

"I figured we'd watch them together. That way, when you get scared, I can hold you."

The chances of Aliyah becoming scared were nonexistent. She'd seen the movies so many times she could act them out herself.

Ethan tilted her chin upward. "How are you feeling now? Do you feel safe in my arms?"

"Yes, but I'd much rather you did more than hold me." She brushed her lips against his.

"What exactly did you have in mind?"

Aliyah smiled and caressed the front of his pants. Over the past two months, she had developed a hearty obsession with Ethan's dick and had no problem letting him know. "We should pick up where we left off last night."

"You want to do the horizontal shuffle again, huh?"

"I do. Along with the vertical and any other angle you'd like to explore."

Ethan leaned in for a kiss as he removed the bag from her hand and set it on the counter. His mouth left hers only for a second to pull his shirt over his head.

Unable to keep her hands to herself, Aliyah swiped them across Ethan's chest and pinched one of his nipples.

"Come here, girl!"

She yelped when he lifted her onto the counter, then licked her lips with expectation as he spread her legs and squeezed her inner thighs.

"I love when you wear a dress."

"Why is that, sir?"

"It gives me easy access to my pussy."

"*Your* pussy?"

"Are you telling me otherwise? Cause if you are, we have a problem."

"What if I am?—Aaah!" she shrieked when he pulled her to the edge of the counter.

"Lay back," he commanded as he removed her panties.

The contact of his mouth on her thigh made Aliyah close her eyes. She inhaled deeply when his tongue replaced his lips, and he moved toward what belonged to him. He took his time at first, but then, as always, his greed won.

"Yes, baby! Eat your pussy!" Aliyah screamed, coming on Ethan's tongue.

When her legs shook, he grabbed them both. Every inch of his girth entered her with force. "Mine!"

"Yours!"

As he administered deep thrusts, he pulled her up. The height of the counter put them both at eye level. "Kiss me, Buttercup. Taste how sweet *my* pussy gets."

Aliyah locked her legs around Ethan and tasted the sweet nectar she made for only him. Moments later, she was lifted and carried to the living room, where he laid her on the sofa. His strokes hit deeper and hungrier there.

"Whose pussy is this?"

"Yours!"

"Can I have it anytime I want it?"

"Yes!—take it!" Aliyah bucked underneath him. Like a volcano, another orgasm erupted.

Ethan gripped her waist tight. His mouth overpowered hers as he came inside her. "That was supposed to last longer," he admitted, laying soft kisses on her face and neck. "How about an encore inside the shower?"

"Mmm," she uttered, then nodded.

Ethan chuckled. "Come on, Buttercup. I'll carry you."

Showers with Ethan always rejuvenated Aliyah; this one was no different. Dressed in his t-shirt and a pair of his sweatpants, she sat on the sofa in the living room while he prepared their popcorn. They were about to start their *Friday the 13th* binge.

"Buttercup, your phone is ringing," Ethan called from the kitchen.

Aliyah had forgotten she'd left it there on the counter. By the time she reached the kitchen, the phone had stopped.

"You want salt and butter on the popcorn?"

"Butter, yes. Salt, no." Aliyah unlocked her phone and pulled down the notification screen. The missed call was from her dad.

"Hey, are you ready to pretend to be scared?"

Ethan asked, walking up behind her.

Stillness consumed Aliyah as she remembered her failed attempt to call her dad.

"What's the matter?"

"Nothing."

Ethan set the bowl of popcorn on the counter. "Don't tell me nothing. You're standing here like a frozen fish dinner."

Aliyah glanced at her phone, then back at Ethan. "Do you remember how I told you my dad left when I was twelve?"

"Yeah."

"I haven't seen or heard from him since. Recently, he's been trying to contact me." Aliyah sat on the bar stool, and Ethan sat next to her. "My mom wants me to forgive him. She wants us to work things out."

Ethan rubbed his hand up and down Aliyah's back.

"I can't bring myself to do it." She shook her head. "I know that sounds ridiculous. I'm twenty-seven, and I still have daddy issues but—"

Ethan leaned forward and placed a finger on Aliyah's lips. He brought her into his arms, and she laid her head on his chest. "My dad and I didn't always agree, either. We stopped communicating for almost two years."

As Ethan spoke and brushed the top of her head with his fingers, Aliyah felt her tension ease.

"Although my dad hated to admit he was wrong, he finally apologized. A month later, we learned he had stage four lung cancer."

Aliyah sat up and looked at Ethan.

"My mom went from planning his sixty-fifth birthday party to planning his funeral."

"I'm so sorry." She laid a hand on the side of Ethan's face, and he covered it with his own.

"Knowing he and I were on good terms had been the one thing that gave me peace," Ethan revealed. "Sometimes, it's not about who's right; it's about doing the right thing."

Aliyah lowered her head as she thought about the mini stroke her father had recently suffered.

"Give it some time before you make your final decision," Ethan advised.

"Okay." Aliyah forced a half-smile and nodded.

"Are you still game for movie night?" He asked as he stroked the side of her face. "We could watch them some other day."

"And miss out on cuddling next to you? No thanks."

They made it to part five when Aliyah's eyelids grew heavy. "I better go."

"Spend the night."

Aliyah lifted her head from Ethan's lap. "I have nothing here to wear in the morning."

Ethan brought her closer and bit the side of her neck. She moaned softly as his lips almost broke through her defenses.

"Is that a yes?"

"I have to start early tomorrow."

"You start work early every day."

Aliyah poked a finger into his chest and stood. All the while, she hoped he wouldn't push the issue.

"Don't you want to take these with you?" Ethan tried to hand her the DVDs.

"No, I'd rather leave them here. We can finish them together, and you can keep me safe."

"Always." He kissed her once more and followed it with a bear hug. "Let's get you home, Buttercup."

*D*ouble dates, weekend rendezvouses, and lots of pillow talk; that's what Ethan's life had become. He wasn't complaining, not one bit. Now and then, he thought of telling Aliyah about Hillary, but pushed the notion away. He hadn't heard from her since the day she showed up drunk at his penthouse. If Hillary tried to contact him, she hadn't been successful. Ethan wasn't complaining about that either.

From inside his custom walk-in closet, he picked out something to wear. As he examined the room, he noted the extra space. Ethan recalled how every time he'd tried to convince Aliyah to stay, she used the excuse of not having clothes at his place. He needed to change that.

At six-thirty, Ethan arrived at Aliyah's modern ranch-style home. With bold, earthy colors, fine lines, and stone accents, the house represented its owner well. Ethan admired that about Aliyah. Her strength, beauty, and drive. All unmatched by any woman he'd ever met.

He rang the doorbell and waited for her to answer. When she did, he couldn't hide his excitement.

"Hi." Aliyah leaned into his kiss while she fastened her earring. "Come in. I'm almost ready."

Ethan smiled as she hurried along. He followed as she walked toward her bedroom and continued to get ready. "Take your time. Our reservation is for seven. I'm sure Drew and Jasmine haven't left their suite yet."

"How do you know them again?" Aliyah asked from inside the closet.

Ethan sat on her bed and picked up the purse that

lay across the plush comforter. "I met them in Dubai. They stayed in my hotel for their honeymoon. Drew and I discussed some business—"

"On their honeymoon!" Aliyah interrupted, walking back into the bedroom.

"Hey, when creativity strikes, take advantage. Anyway, we kept in touch. Recently, he bought into one of my investments."

"So, he's a business partner?"

"And a friend. This looks familiar," Ethan said, holding up her gold chain-linked purse.

"I wore it the night you seduced me in Jamaica."

Ethan stood and walked over to Aliyah. He wrapped his hands around her waist. "It is you who seduced me, and you still are." He laid a soft peck on her lips. "We better go, or we *will* be late."

Other than Xavier—who was more like a brother, despite the obvious difference in their race—Ethan didn't have many friends, and he preferred it that way. Drew and he had connected because they were much alike. Ethan respected him. Not just because of his success, but his ability to not let the past ruin his future with Jasmine.

Ethan wanted someone he could trust, marry, have children, and grow old with. He thought about how Aliyah's distaste for marriage loomed over their relationship. He wondered if she would ever change her mind. Maybe after she saw how well Drew and Jasmine's marriage worked.

They'd been through a lot, yet still, they were a powerful unit.

When they arrived at Aromas, the hostess escorted them to the private dining room. Drew and Jasmine stood as they entered.

"Jasmine, your new credentials look amazing on you," Ethan said before he kissed her cheek. He and Drew shook hands and patted each other on the back. "I'd like you both to meet my beautiful girlfriend, Aliyah ... Buttercup, this is Drew and Jasmine Watts."

As Aliyah shook their hands, Ethan took note of how Jasmine lit up. The two women were so much alike. Independent, strong, and sexy. They didn't need a man. A man needed them.

"You're gorgeous," Jasmine said.

"Wow! Thank you. I was thinking the same about you," Aliyah bashfully admitted.

"How about you two gorgeous women have a seat?" Drew teased.

"Jasmine, how does it feel to be an MD?"

"Exhausting," she said with a chuckle. "How are things going with the ski resort?"

Ethan faced Aliyah. "She can tell you better than me."

Jasmine looked at them, confused.

"I'm the project manager," Aliyah said. "Things are going well. We have all our permits, and we've passed every inspection. We're looking to break ground around April."

"That's four months away," Drew said.

"Beautiful and smart. Is that how you two met?" Jasmine asked.

Once again, Ethan eyed Aliyah. He figured he'd let her tell the story.

"No, we met this past July in Jamaica. I was on vacation with my friends, and we stayed at Ethan's hotel."

"We had a minor mishap, but all became better after I apologized," Ethan added. Underneath the table, he squeezed Aliyah's leg, and she jumped.

"Uh-huh," Jasmine said. "Well, Drew and I would love to invite you both to our house in Aspen for Christmas. That's if you don't have plans."

Ethan wanted to expose Aliyah to a *positive* marriage, mainly since Drew and Jasmine weren't much older than them. "I don't see why not." He looked at Aliyah, knowing he had the advantage of three against one.

"No, I don't have plans. However, I need to tie up some loose ends at the office before I leave. How long will you be at your home in Aspen?" Aliyah asked.

"A week. If you're able to come, you'll meet our

son, Drew Jr.," Jasmine said.

"Yeah, I think I can spare a week. I've heard it's beautiful there, especially during the holidays."

"Great!" Jasmine cheered.

Drew poured champagne in everyone's glass, then held up his. "To Aspen."

A sense of achievement moved through Ethan. Things between him and Aliyah were better than he ever imagined.

Over dinner, the four discussed their busy lives and told jokes. Drew and Jasmine shared their story with Aliyah. Ethan watched as tears welled in her eyes, and she blinked them away.

"I think it's time for a bathroom break," Aliyah said.

"I'll join you." Jasmine stood with her, and they walked toward the bathroom.

"So," Drew said once the women left.

"So," Ethan echoed.

Drew laughed. "Buttercup, huh? Dude, you got it bad."

"Whatever, man."

"Hey." Drew held up his hands. "I'm not judging. I'm just calling it like I see it."

"What about you? You don't have it bad?"

"I never said I didn't."

Ethan nodded. "Right. What should I do?"

"Have you told her how you feel?"

"You mean have I told her I love her? No, I haven't. It's complicated."

"I know all about that."

Ethan took a deep breath. "I haven't told her about Hillary."

"I see." Drew motioned for the waiter that stood in the corner.

"Yes, sir?"

"Bring us a bottle of Hennessy and two glasses with two cubes of ice in each." Drew turned his attention back to Ethan. "I won't tell you what to do, but I will tell you this. That woman loves you."

Ethan stilled and met Drew's gaze.

"Rather she's told you or not, she does."

Ethan shook his head. All the advancements he'd made with Aliyah felt like nothing. The minute she found out about Hillary, she would leave him.

Aliyah stared at herself in the mirror as she washed her hands. On the outside, she appeared tranquil, but internally she was a tangled ball of yarn. Conflicted with her thoughts and feelings, she felt like a caged bird desperate to escape. She wanted what Jasmine and Drew had. Their story was inspiring. Despite what they'd gone through, they survived and remained together.

Jasmine didn't lose herself. She kept her practice and furthered her education to become a doctor. Aliyah's mind drifted to her thoughts of becoming an architect. Could she have it all, too? The sexy husband. The career. What about children? Did Ethan want children?

"Aliyah?"

"Huh?"

"You've been scrubbing your hands for a while there," Jasmine said.

Aliyah examined her hands submerged underneath the water. "Oh." She turned off the faucet and grabbed a few paper towels. "I got a little distracted."

"It happens. Anything I can help with?"

Aliyah shook her head.

"Are you sure?"

Aliyah studied her reflection once more, then faced Jasmine. "I know it hasn't been easy for you and Drew. I'm sure you deal with your normal issues."

Jasmine walked closer and laid her hand on Aliyah's shoulder. "I understand. You've been hurt. You took a chance on Ethan, and you can't afford to be wrong."

"He came out of nowhere," Aliyah said, in disbelief.

"They usually do ... You love him, don't you?"

Aliyah glanced at the floor. "I can't answer that question, not yet."

"Understandable. Just so you know, he's in love with you."

"He told you that!" Mixed emotions swarmed in as Aliyah's eyes widened.

"No, but one only has to look to see." Jasmine smiled. "Love is complicated sometimes."

All this talk about love caused Aliyah's head to spin. It had been hard to admit she liked Ethan. Now, she had to admit she loved him?

"How about we save this talk for another day?" Jasmine recommended.

"Good idea."

With her new friend, Aliyah walked back into the dining room.

Chapter Fourteen

December~

Seasons change, and so do people. Aliyah attested to that. As the new year peeked around the corner, she thought about the changes within herself and her life. This had been the first Thanksgiving and Christmas she celebrated separately from her mom. With her mom and Rob constantly traveling, Aliyah had to readjust her plans.

In the beginning, she struggled with her decision to go to Aspen. Aliyah feared things with Ethan were progressing too fast, but her worries subsided after spending Christmas with him and the Watts. One week with Drew and Jasmine had resuscitated Aliyah's belief in marriage.

Seated in her car, she adjusted the volume of the radio. She and Ethan had arrived back in Seattle that Monday morning. Aliyah wasn't supposed to return to work until Tuesday, but Ethan had an issue that required his attention. Not wanting to lounge around the house all day, she headed to Mills.

At the office, Aliyah prepped for the week. She answered emails and returned calls—including personal ones.

"About time," Amanda blasted Aliyah over the phone.

"I'm sorry, I've been busy."

"Yeah, yeah. When are you going to have time for your friends?"

"Don't act like that."

"No, *you* don't act like that. You're the main one who talks about not forgetting your friends because of a man."

"I didn't forget anyone. I told you, I've been busy."

"You can tell us everything over dinner tonight."

Dread washed over Aliyah. She had made plans with Ethan. If she told Amanda that, she would prove her right. "Sure, I'll be there."

"Is Mr. Sexy coming too?"

The flirtatious tone in Amanda's voice made Aliyah roll her eyes upward. "No, just me."

"Are you afraid to bring him around?"

Aliyah shook her head. She had nothing to worry about with Amanda or any of her friends. Amanda was simply being Amanda. "No. If you're done telling me how awful of a friend I am, I'm going to finish my work so I can leave on time."

"I didn't say that."

"No, but you insinuated."

"Always the victim."

"Whatever, bye!"

After she hung up, Aliyah became caught up in Amanda's accusations. Guilt ate at her. Had she forgotten about her friends? Had she sacrificed them to nurture her relationship with Ethan?

Aliyah went through the calendar on her phone, and calculated the last time she met up with Amanda and the others.

October?

In shock, she shook her head. She had turned into the friend she despised.

Aliyah:
Hey, I have to meet with the girls.
I might be a little late.
Delivered: 3:00 PM.

Ethan:
No problem.
I'm still at the office.
Call me when you're on the way.
Received: 3:01 PM.

Aliyah:
Okay.
Delivered: 3:02PM.

Later that evening, Aliyah walked through the doors of *Capital Grille* and prepared herself for the worst.

"Are my eyes deceiving me, or am I seeing Aliyah Carter?" Tina said, sitting in the seat across from her.

"Last time I checked, Amanda was the dramatic one in the group," Aliyah bit back.

"Whatever," Amanda hissed. "At least I didn't go missing for two months."

Three sets of eyes turned Aliyah's way.

"She has a point, Liya," Serena said.

"Wow. The three of you are ganging up on me?" Aliyah nodded. "It's cool. I deserve this. I should have been a better friend and made time for you guys." She blew out a breath. "Between preparations for the ski resort and attending events with Ethan, my time has been scarce."

They all remained quiet and continued to stare at her.

"Every week last month, we went to some type of event. We just came back from Aspen, and this weekend, we are attending his cousin's New Year's Eve housewarming party."

"Do you hear yourself?"

Aliyah wore a dumbfounded expression as she

faced Amanda. "What?"

"You sound like the pig that went wee wee wee, all the way home." Amanda laughed, and Serena joined her.

"You both need to stop," Tina said. She reached across the table and patted Aliyah's hand. "I mean, it's obvious you're brushing up on your French."

Aliyah raised a brow. "My French?"

"Wee."

Laughter filled the air once more, and this time, Aliyah joined them.

"But on a serious note, we're happy for you. You look like a woman—"

"In love," Serena finished Tina's sentence.

"Is it love?" Amanda asked with curiosity.

Over the last three and a half months, Aliyah hadn't used the word, and neither had Ethan. She'd only discussed her feelings with Jasmine.

Aliyah searched her heart. Was love indeed what she felt for him? She and Ethan had passed the phase where their attraction was fueled by only lust, desires, and physical appearances.

On several occasions, they'd enjoyed each other's company without it leading to sex. They'd filled their conversations with more than sexual innuendos and flirtatious remarks. They were supportive and nurturing toward one another.

Unsure of how to respond, she looked over at her

friends, who were waiting for an answer. "I don't know, but I am the happiest I've been in a long time."

Awws echoed around the table.

"I want to apologize for the crap I've given you all. My bitter rants about men probably drove you crazy."

"Girl, don't worry about it. That's what friends are for. We listened to each other's problems, and we have each other's back," Tina said.

Aliyah knew Tina's words rang true for more than one reason. They were the only two that knew she and Ben had gone through a break-up. "I appreciate all three of you."

"Since we've kissed and made up, can we talk about this gorgeous new mane Amanda is sporting?" Serena asked.

Amanda batted her lashes and flipped her hair. "She arrived yesterday. I ordered her online."

Aliyah combed her fingers through the silky strands. "How much?"

"Five hundred," Amanda replied without so much as a blink.

"What!" Aliyah's eyes widened.

Amanda swayed her head from side to side. "Some of us aren't lucky enough to have fast-growing hair like you and these two chicks."

Aliyah ignored her comment. She was in a good

mood and determined to keep it that way.

"You should see all the attention she gets me." Amanda continued.

Tina snorted. "As if you need more."

"What's that supposed to mean?"

"It means you attract enough attention with that big ass you're sitting on."

"Facts!" Aliyah said, as she gave Tina a hi-five.

Amanda aimed her gaze at Tina. "Whatever. I'm not the one walking around poking my chest out in everyone's face."

"I do not! I can't help it. Big breasts run in my family!"

After the women's laughter subsided, Serena cleared her throat. "What about me?"

"Oh, honey, did we leave you out?" Amanda teased.

Serena squinted but didn't respond.

"We wouldn't leave you out. You know how much I wish I had your eyes."

Serena smiled.

"Yes, honey! If I had those green beauties, I would pull all kinds of sugar daddies—I'm talking every flava." Amanda snapped her fingers and flipped her hair for the third time. Her actions caused them all to laugh again.

New Year's Eve~

Ethan:
How much longer? I miss you.
Delivered: 6:42 PM.

Aliyah:
Parking now! I miss you too.
Received: 6:43 PM.

The more time Ethan spent with Aliyah, the more he changed. He wasn't an unaffectionate man, but he didn't cuddle, and he certainly didn't tell women he missed them—except his mom. With Aliyah, he didn't know how not to do those things. She brought out his nurturing side.

As he stood inside his closet, he anticipated Aliyah's reaction. For the first time, he considered the possibility of her hating his surprise. Ethan decided he'd wait until after Kimberly and Xavier's party to show her.

He turned out the closet's light and stepped back

into his bedroom. From his bed, he collected his suit jacket, then walked toward the kitchen. He poured himself a much-needed shot.

At the sound of soft knocks, Ethan headed toward the living room. The second he opened the door, he fell harder for the woman who stood on the other side.

"You make a man lose all train of thought; you know that?"

Aliyah walked inside and wrapped her arms around his neck. "Doing what I can, with what I got."

"You got a lot, and I want all of it." Ethan's hand traveled down the black sequin dress she wore. He squeezed her ass, then moved back up to the zipper.

"Hey! Stop that!" Playfully, she pushed him away.

"We have time." Ethan moved closer and pulled her into his arms for another embrace.

"No, we don't. Besides, it's rude to be late."

"It's Kimberly and Xavier."

Aliyah stood on her tiptoes and kissed Ethan on the lips. "Don't worry. I'll make it up to you when we get home."

Home. Such a simple word. Yet, it insinuated so much. He knew Aliyah hadn't meant it the way he'd taken it, but the thought of them living together didn't sound so bad. *One day.* Ethan released her. He retrieved his blazer from the kitchen and returned.

"All set."

For most of the drive, they both remained quiet. Only the sounds of old-school R&B filled Ethan's Bentley Continental GT. A few times, he glimpsed in Aliyah's direction. His new mood had affected her; he needed to say something. "How was your day?"

"Not bad. Yours?"

"Stressful." Ethan reached over and gently squeezed Aliyah's thigh. The feel of her delicate fingers on top of his hand put a smile on his face. "It's better now. Much better."

When they pulled up to Kimberly and Xavier's new house, many cars were parked. After exiting his coupe, Ethan came around and opened the passenger's door for Aliyah.

"The exterior is beautiful!" Aliyah said.

Ethan took in the massive two-story red brick waterfront, Tudor. A mixture of Victorian and classical, the structure certainly got your attention. He faced Aliyah once more and smiled at the gleam in her eyes. "If I know Kimberly, the inside is just as impressive."

Together, they walked toward the front door. Seconds after Ethan knocked and rang the doorbell, Xavier answered.

"My two favorite people, come in."

"I thought you said the guest list was small?" Ethan mentioned as they followed Xavier through the foyer.

"You know how Kimberly is. Once she gets going, she can't stop."

"Where *is* my lovely cousin?"

"She's around here somewhere. Probably in the kitchen."

"Then we'll give this to you." Ethan handed Xavier a navy blue and gold-wrapped package.

"What's this?"

"Your housewarming gift."

Xavier shifted the package in his hand. "Thanks, man. You didn't have to buy us anything."

"It wasn't my idea."

"I should have known you wouldn't have done something so considerate on your own."

"I do considerate things all the time."

"I disagree," Kimberly said, walking up from the side.

"Look, honey. They brought us a housewarming gift."

"Thanks, Aliyah."

"He said 'they brought.'"

Kimberly ignored Ethan and approached Aliyah. "It's good to see you again."

"Thank you. It's good to see you too."

"Hey, Ethan. Do you have a minute? I need to

show you something."

"You agreed not to work today," Kimberly said, reminding Xavier of his promise.

"Five minutes."

"Fine. Aliyah and I have some catching up to do."

The thought of Aliyah being left alone with Kimberly didn't sit right with Ethan. He knew his cousin. If given a chance, she would say something that he'd be left to explain.

"*Everything* seems to be coming along with Cedar Peak," Kimberly said, as she handed Aliyah a flute of champagne.

"Yes, it is." Aliyah shook her head in disbelief. "I still can't believe Ethan gave me free rein over the design process."

"I can." Kimberly wore a knowing smirk.

"Were we that obvious?"

"You, not so much, but Ethan has never been able to keep anything from me."

"The two of you must be very close."

Kimberly looked over the rim of her glass in Ethan's and Xavier's direction. "Like any cousins, but

I have the inside scoop."

"Right. What's it like working with him?"

"Who? Ethan?"

"Yeah."

"It's not so bad. His expectations are higher because we're related."

"You two behave more like siblings than you do cousins."

Kimberly chuckled. "I actually have four older brothers. I'm the only girl in a family full of boys."

"I don't have any siblings. I'm an only child."

"Ethan has a younger brother," Kimberly mentioned.

Aliyah nodded. "I'm excited to meet him in February."

"Oh, Ethan is taking you to Paris?"

"Yes."

"You'll love Alex. He's such a sweetheart—ooh, before I forget." Kimberly touched Aliyah's arm. "Tell Ethan to take you to Café de brûlée."

Aliyah nodded. "I'll make sure he adds it to our itinerary."

Out of the corner of her eye, Aliyah saw Ethan and Xavier returning. They were still discussing business, but Aliyah spotted an exchange between Kimberly and Ethan. She couldn't decipher what it meant, and her bladder was posing as a distraction.

"Kimberly, which way is your bathroom? This

champagne has worked its way through me."

"Come on. I'll show you."

The urge to look back at Ethan gnawed at Aliyah. Something was up with him. His demeanor had changed at the penthouse. He shifted from relaxed to preoccupied. Had she once again made a mistake? Had she put herself out there only to be hurt again?

Aliyah followed Kimberly through the maze of her house. "Every aspect of your home is breathtaking," she complimented.

"Thank you. The renovations took longer than expected, but I am pleased with the finished results. ... How are you?"

"I'm good. Why do you ask?"

Kimberly shrugged. "No particular reason. I've become fond of you—if you don't mind me saying."

Aliyah smiled. "Not at all. I'm fond of you, too."

"Well, here we are," Kimberly announced.

"Wow!" Aliyah peeked inside the exquisite, luxurious bathroom. "You're going to have to give me the grand tour of your entire house."

Kimberly laughed. "With pleasure. Do you want me to wait, or can you find your way back?"

"I think I can manage," Aliyah said, before disappearing into the bathroom.

Chapter Fifteen

The moment Ethan spotted Kimberly returning, he knew she was about to stir the pot.

"Have you told her about Hillary?"

Ethan looked around Kimberly for Aliyah. "No."

"Why not?"

"Aliyah doesn't need to know about her."

"She does, and it needs to come from you."

"Hillary is long gone. She doesn't matter anymore." Ethan adjusted his collar. "She never did."

"I agree—about the last part. But you and I both know Hillary will slither her way back into your life."

"Not this time."

Unconvinced, Kimberly pressed. "Aliyah still has the right to know—"

"I have the right to know what?"

"How beautiful you are, and how I'm the luckiest man in the room."

Aliyah blushed.

"My dear cousin was scolding me for not giving you a tour of her and Xavier's lovely new home." Ethan held up his arm. "Shall we?"

"Yes."

On the ride back to his place, Ethan mulled over Kimberly's words. The competent part of him knew Aliyah had a right to know the truth. Still, his selfish side didn't want to jeopardize what they had.

"Hey, what's on your mind?" Aliyah asked.

Ethan glanced in her direction. "Huh?"

"You're deep in thought."

"Oh, I was planning a seduction."

"Surely, you're not out of tricks, Mr. Phillips? It wouldn't take much."

"Hmm? If I asked you to spend the night, would you?" Ethan figured this to be the perfect time to set the stage for her surprise.

"Are we there yet?"

"My place?"

"No. The point where we spend the night at each other's home."

"I wasn't aware there was a timeline." Once again, his doubt returned. Had he made the wrong move?

They rode in the elevator and walked down the hall in silence.

Ethan unlocked his door and moved forward, but Aliyah's feet remained planted where they were.

"What's wrong?" he asked.

"You tell me. You're the one who's acting strange."

Ethan placed his keys inside his pocket. "Nothing is wrong." He concluded that wasn't the correct answer when she turned to leave. "Where are you going?"

"Home."

"Why?"

Aliyah wiggled out of his grasp. "I'm tired and sleepy."

"Sleep here."

"I can't. I have to work today."

"It's Saturday, and it's New Year's."

"Michael and I work on New Year's. We go over the new projects and plan them out on the whiteboard in his office. It's quite productive since everyone else is out."

Ethan shook his head. They were getting off-topic. He re-approached Aliyah and grabbed her hands once more. "Come here. I want to show you something." Inside, he led her to his bedroom and over to his walk-in closet.

"What's in here? Other than your clothes?"

"You'll see in a second." Ethan turned on the light

and pulled her into the spacious, organized room. He nodded to the right side of the wardrobe.

Aliyah covered her mouth and moved closer to get a better view. Unable to resist, she reached out to stroke a dress.

"There's more over here."

Aliyah turned around and eyed the drawers Ethan had opened. Not only had he given her space in his closet, but he'd supplied the clothes as well.

"I, I don't know what to say."

From behind, Ethan wrapped his hands around her waist. "Say you'll spend the night."

"I can't." Once more, she wiggled out of his embrace and headed back into the bedroom.

"Why?"

"I have my reasons." Aliyah sighed as she walked over to the bed and sat.

Ethan grabbed her hand and brought her attention back to him. He turned her slightly, so they faced each other. "Which are?"

Aliyah tilted her head to the side, refusing to make eye contact. "When you spend the night, real-life starts." She pressed her lips together. "You start feeling things for the other person."

"That usually happens over time, regardless if you spend the night. What exactly don't you want to feel?"

Aliyah pulled her hand away. "I'm afraid, Ethan.

Is that what you want me to say?"

He moved closer and caressed her face. "No. It's not." Ethan wiped the single tear off her cheek. "Buttercup, what's wrong?"

"Lorenzo."

"We don't have to talk about him."

"We do."

Ethan didn't want to hear about another man, but he figured this trip down memory lane was necessary to work through their issue. "Whatever you want."

She took a deep breath, then spoke. "I met him while on a business trip to New York. We dated for a year. At first, I was against the idea of long-distance dating, but we made it work. Things got pretty serious between us, to the point I contemplated a job offer in New York."

Ethan clenched his jaw. He could tell he wouldn't like this story.

"I hadn't told him or anyone else about the job. I wanted to surprise him." Aliyah wiped her cheek. "After my interview, I went to his office. I should have known something was wrong. His receptionist was far too nice that day; she allowed me to go back without hesitation."

"I got halfway to his office when I heard a child giggling. Lorenzo's voice came next, followed by a woman. She asked if he was coming home or staying in the city that night. The little girl repeated the question. He told them both he was coming home."

Aliyah looked down at her hands. "When I stepped forward, Lorenzo was kissing the woman—his wife. I ran out of there ... but I didn't leave New York."

Ethan's forehead creased. He studied Aliyah as she stared off into the distance.

"I waited for him to leave work, and I followed him home—his real home. I spied on them for almost an hour." Aliyah covered her face. "You must think I'm pathetic."

Ethan pulled her into his arms. "No, you were hurting." He rocked her back and forth. "That will not happen with us. I have other homes, but you can visit them all."

Aliyah chuckled.

"Stay with me tonight."

"Technically, it's morning."

Ethan smiled and kissed the top of her head. "Will you stay?"

"Yes."

Waking up next to Aliyah had been something Ethan desired since their first night together in Jamaica. Other than that one night at his cabin, she always ran away, but not this time. He'd captured her and planned never to let her go. Ethan hated to see her in pain. Kimberly was right. Aliyah deserved the truth; today, he would tell her.

Ethan ran his fingers down her arm, causing her to stir.

"Good morning."

"That it is. Did you sleep well?"

Aliyah sat up and leaned on her elbow. "Yes, I did."

"See. That wasn't so bad."

"No, it wasn't. What time is it?"

"Almost ten. Spend the day with me."

"I have a job to go to."

Ethan stroked her arm once more. "True, but your job consists of you working as the project manager for my ski resort. That means you work for me. Since I'm the boss, I'm giving you the day off."

"I'm more than positive it doesn't work like that."

"Today it will."

Aliyah's eyes rolled toward the ceiling. "Spend one night at a man's house, and suddenly, he owns you."

"Suddenly?"

"Welp, that's my cue. Time to go." Aliyah shifted

to get up.

"I'm joking." Ethan leaned forward and gave her a peck on the lips. "Please, spend the day with me, or at least, the rest of the morning."

"I guess I can go in later today. I need to let Michael know. He has probably tried to call me by now."

Ethan smiled. He thought for sure she would make him work harder.

"First, I need a shower, followed by coffee and breakfast," she stated her demands.

"Sounds reasonable. You shower, and I'll work on the other two." He kissed her once more, then hopped out of bed.

Inside the kitchen, Ethan got to work. He prepared the waffle batter, then fired up the waffle maker. While the bacon seared in one pan, and he scrambled eggs in another, *Sade's 'Smooth Operator'* played throughout the penthouse.

Aliyah emerged as he removed the first waffle from the machine. "Looks like you're having fun in here."

Ethan refilled the waffle maker, then shimmied Aliyah's way. He tugged on his t-shirt and pulled the drawstring to the sweatpants she had also borrowed. Despite the closet full of clothes he'd bought her, she'd chosen this to wear. "You like wearing my clothes."

Aliyah slid her hands up around his neck. "You don't mind, do you?"

"Not one bit." He lowered his face and pulled her bottom lip into his mouth.

"Careful, you might burn the waffles."

"I have more batter," Ethan said, before brushing his lips over her neck and ear.

Aliyah chuckled and peeked over her shoulder. "Um, it sounds like someone's at your door."

"Here, take over. You know how to work one of these, right?"

"Honey, I'm the queen of making waffles—among other things."

Ethan raised a brow. "When I come back, we'll discuss those other things."

Aliyah stuck out her tongue and poured more batter into the waffle maker.

As Ethan crossed the living room, he wondered who was at his door. Kimberly and Xavier were most likely still in bed. He'd spoken to his mother the other day and made plans for Aliyah to meet her that following weekend. The two had talked over the phone but never met in person.

Unprepared was an understatement for what Ethan felt when he opened the door. "How the fuck did you get up here?"

Hillary ignored Ethan's harsh words and moved past him. "Good morning. I hope I didn't wake you. I was in the neighborhood, and I figured I'd stop by."

"I asked you a question," he said through gritted teeth.

"I had to climb the gate and sneak in through the garage. That damn guard practically threw me in the bushes!—I should sue his ass!"

"You do, and I'll sue you for trespassing!"

Hillary gripped her hips. "I wouldn't have to go through such drastic measures if you would take my calls." She combed a hand through her unruly hair and flipped it over her shoulder. "I'm in trouble, Ethan. I need your help."

"Not. My. Fucking. Problem. Get out!" Ethan grabbed Hillary's arm and pulled her toward the door.

"Ethan, you're hurting me!"

"This is how I deal with people who barge their way into my house!"

"Listen—"

Ethan cut her words off by squeezing her arm.

"Ow!"

"Leave!"

"All right! I'm going!"

At the sound of Aliyah's voice, both Ethan and Hillary turned around.

"Shit!" he muttered.

Hillary's gaze shifted between Ethan and Aliyah. "Oh! Who do we have here? Is *she* the reason you want me to leave?"

"I'm warning you!"

"Calm down." Hillary headed in Aliyah's direction with her hand outstretched. "Hi, I'm Hillary. Ethan's wife."

"Wife?" Aliyah dropped her hand.

"Ex-wife!" he corrected, not missing the glare Aliyah sent his way.

Hillary smirked. "Sorry, it's still a habit. Our divorce has only been final for a few months."

"Leave before I throw you out the fucking window!" Ethan barked.

Hillary's eyes widened. "He's such a temperamental creature. Very aggressive—if you know what I mean." She smiled smugly, then walked out.

Ethan closed the door. With caution, he turned back around and faced Aliyah. He saw the fire in her eyes. He'd betrayed her. As he approached, she backed away, decreasing his advances.

"When were you going to tell me about your wife?"

"She's not my—"

"Oh, I'm sorry, ex-wife." Aliyah shook her head. "You said you've never been married."

"I didn't use those words."

"No, you didn't. You just allowed me to believe that."

"What was I supposed to do? You despise marriage, and you leave no room for mistakes!"

"You're saying this is my fault? Are you serious?" Aliyah scoffed. "Go to hell!" She walked around to the other side of the table.

"Wait!" Ethan grabbed her arm, but she snatched it away from him.

"There are three things I don't play about. My mom, my heart, and my career. Right now, you're a threat to the last two."

Ethan thrust his hands into the pockets of his jeans. "I fucked up!" he confessed with raised shoulders.

Aliyah folded her arms across her chest. "Were you married when we slept together in Jamaica?"

He could only stare at her.

"I thought so."

"Please, let me explain."

"You had plenty of time to do that!"

Crippled by his idiocy, Ethan remained where he stood and watched Aliyah walk out the door.

Chapter Sixteen

Downstairs in the garage, Aliyah sat in her car. In a fit of rage, she banged her fist against the steering wheel. "Stupid, stupid, stupid!"

Her head throbbed, and her heartbeat echoed in her throat. "Not again! This shit can't be happening again!" She wanted to cry. She wanted to go back upstairs and punch Ethan in the face. Hard.

She needed a diversion. Aliyah pressed the start button, turned *Whitney Houston* up, and drove to work.

"What are you wearing?"

"They're called sweatpants. They were invented in the nineteen-twenties."

When Michael tilted his head to the side, Aliyah knew he'd seen through her attempt to display her usual sassy, insubordinate behavior.

"I thought you weren't coming in until—"

"Change of plans. Give me a minute, and I'll come to your office." She turned her back to him and arranged things on her desk. "By the way, you can assign me more projects."

"What did he do?"

"Nothing. Everything is fine." Seconds passed, and she felt Michael's hand on her shoulder.

"Do I need to break his nose?"

Aliyah forced herself not to laugh. The thought of Michael willing to jeopardize a multi-million-dollar contract made her smile. "No." She gave his hand a reassuring tap.

"What about his account? Do I need to re-assign it to someone else?"

She shook her head. "That won't be necessary." Aliyah could still do her job without running into Ethan. Also, she didn't want her colleagues in her business.

"If that changes, let me know." He removed his hand from her shoulder and turned to leave.

"Michael?"

"Yeah?"

"You're the big brother I always wanted."

Michael chuckled. "You're the little sister I never knew I needed."

At nine o'clock, Aliyah pulled into her garage.

Ethan had texted and called throughout the day, but she refused to respond. There was nothing left to say. Once again, she'd slept with another woman's husband. Aliyah considered herself intelligent. Yet, she couldn't choose the right man. Perhaps she was meant to be alone.

She leaned her head back against the headrest and analyzed her life. At twenty-seven, she had become a millionaire; and landed a six-figure career. What was her secret to success? She hadn't let a man complicate her life.

She'd seen what happened when you let love take over. Aliyah thought of her mother and how she had given her father twenty-five of her best years. Only to have him leave her for a younger woman. She thought of her friends who'd given up their dreams to become wives and mothers.

Memories. That's all they had of their former selves.

Aliyah had decided that would never happen to her. Even if the last four months had been everything she wanted in a relationship. It was a lie—he was a lie.

She became irritated with her thoughts and shook her head. Determined to prevent the tears that threatened to form, she squeezed her eyes shut.

"I will not cry over another man."

Aliyah turned off her car and let the garage door

down. Once inside, she went about her nightly routine and pretended it didn't hurt. That she didn't want to lie in bed, watch *Desperate Housewives,* and binge on a tub of chocolate ice cream.

"No! I will not gain weight for him!"

Aliyah's only plans were to sleep in all day that Saturday. She made a mistake when she told Michael to give her more work that past week. Not only had he assigned her two new clients, but he'd also asked her to help McCallister with his existing accounts.

"I'm coming!" she yelled with anger at the person on the other side of her front door. They prevented her from much-needed rest. On her tiptoes, she used the peephole to identify the culprit. "Mom? Where's your key?" she asked as she unlocked the door.

Kaleen walked inside. "I left it at home. What's going on with you? Michael said you've been off for a week."

"I wasn't off. I worked from home—when did you talk to Michael?"

"A little while ago, at Tidbits. He was there with

his girlfriend—I'm assuming she was his girlfriend."

If Michael and Danita had gone public with their relationship, Aliyah was happy for them.

"Did you forget about our lunch date? Why is it so dark in here?" Kaleen walked over to the bay window and opened the blinds without waiting for answers.

The glare of light made Aliyah cringe. She left her mother's questions unanswered and sat on the sofa.

"What's going on?" Kaleen sat beside her. "Are you sick?"

"No."

Kaleen rubbed Aliyah's back. "Then what's the matter? Are you pregnant?"

"No! I'm tired. I've been working a lot." Aliyah covered her face.

"That's it?"

"Yes."

"Honey, I'm your mother. I know when something is bothering you."

Aliyah held her head. It took a minute, but she finally spoke. "I met his wife, well, his ex-wife."

"Is this about Lorenzo?"

"No, Ethan."

"Oh? How did you find out?"

"She showed up at his house."

"Look on the bright side. At least he's divorced."

"Bright-side? Mom, he wasn't when we first met.

Which means he cheated on his wife! With me!"

"Did he say why?"

"Does it matter? He's a liar. Just like the others."

"You should hear his side of the story."

Aliyah stood and walked toward the center of the room. "Why are you making excuses for him?"

"I'm not making excuses. I just think the two of you should talk."

"There's nothing to talk about. Same song; different station."

"Sweetheart, no one is perfect."

Aliyah shook her head. "Why do you do that?"

"Do what?"

"Take up for men when they're wrong."

Kaleen narrowed her eyes. "I beg your pardon!"

"With Lorenzo, it was 'Maybe they're separated.' Now, with Ethan, it's 'No one is perfect.' Even with my dad—" Aliyah stopped. She wasn't sure if she should share with her mom what she knew.

"What about your dad?"

"I heard you and him arguing the night he left. You begged him to stay. You even tried to use me, but that didn't work. He still left us and started a life with someone else!"

Kaleen looked away.

"You took up for him. You told me I should forgive him. After I heard him say, he had another child on the way. After I heard him say, he didn't want me." Tears trickled down Aliyah's face as she spoke.

"Aliyah, please—"

"You always tell me to forgive people, to move on. I can't!—I won't!"

Kaleen wiped tears from her own face. "I'm sorry if I made you feel that way." She shook her head. "It was my guilt. There are things about me I'm embarrassed for you to find out."

Aliyah watched her mother strangely. "What kind of things?"

"Your father left because I cheated on him."

"What!"

"I was twenty-five when I met David. Your father had gone on his first deployment."

"David? As in David, who you were with after you and dad divorced?"

Kaleen nodded. "We fooled around until Cornelius came back. When I learned I was pregnant with you, I wasn't sure which of them was your father."

Aliyah covered her mouth.

"Once you were born, and I looked into your eyes, in my heart, I knew you belonged to Cornelius."

More tears streamed down Aliyah's face.

"Five years went by, and your father went on another deployment. I ran into David, and we started seeing each other again." Kaleen shook her head and closed her eyes. "I was so weak ... I, I needed someone to talk to."

Kaleen stared blankly at her hands. "Your father found out. I begged for his forgiveness. We went to counseling, and things were getting better. Until your father ran into David."

"Talk about bad luck. They ended up at the same bar that night. A fight broke out between them, and David told Cornelius you weren't his child."

Aliyah sat beside her mom.

"He came home and asked me about it. I told him there was no doubt in my mind you were his. He seemed to take that answer and said we needed a fresh start. He retired from the military, and we moved here."

"I was seven when we moved. You guys didn't divorce until I was twelve."

"Borrowed time," Kaleen said with a shrug. "He forgave me, but he didn't forget—nor did he trust me. I figured he was seeing someone. I didn't know who, but I suspected someone employed by him."

"Stephanie," Aliyah spoke her father's former secretary and wife's name.

"I couldn't be mad. I pushed him toward her. That night, when you heard us arguing, he told me he was leaving me, and he wanted a DNA test for you."

"Oh, mom!"

"Naturally, my infidelity came out during the

divorce process, and they forced me to submit to a DNA test. The test confirmed he was your father, but the damage was done. You hated him." Kaleen squinted. "I never understood why; the two of you were always so close." She smiled at Aliyah sympathetically. "Now I know. It's all my fault."

Aliyah inhaled deeply. "Is this the reason you never married, David?"

"Yes. Out of respect for your father." Kaleen lowered her head. "I know. The irony of it all."

The sound of Aliyah's phone startled them both.

As she wiped tears from her face, Aliyah walked into the kitchen. She didn't recognize the number, but still answered.

"Hello?" Aliyah frowned. The woman on the other end sounded stressed, and Aliyah could tell she'd been crying. "Yes, this is her speaking. Who is this? ... What? Which hospital? ... I'm on my way!" Aliyah hung up the phone and walked toward her bedroom.

"Who was that?" Kaleen asked as she followed. "Aliyah!"

"That was Stephanie. My dad had another stroke. He's in the ICU. I have to go."

"Oh, God! I should come too."

"No." Aliyah laid her hands on the sides of her mother's arms. "I don't think that's a good idea."

Kaleen sniffed and nodded.

"I'll call you once I know more."

"Okay."

Aliyah hugged her mother, then got dressed.

Twenty minutes later, Aliyah parked and rushed toward the hospital's entrance. She thought of every attempt her father had made over the past few months to contact her.

Why was I so cold?

She didn't have all the facts, that's why. She didn't know the depths of the situation. Aliyah rushed down the hall to the elevator. Her fingers trembled as she pressed the button.

There's time. There has to be time.

She stepped into the elevator and rode it to the fifth floor. In a complete fog, she headed to the first nursing station she came across.

"Hi, I'm looking for—"

"Aliyah?"

She turned her head as an ivory-complexion woman approached. Layers of dark brown hair wrapped around the sides of her pretty, worried face. "Yes."

"I'm Stephanie, your father's wife."

Aliyah stared into the woman's teary green eyes and shook her outstretched hand. "How, how is he?"

"He's going in and out. He's been asking for you."

Aliyah glimpsed at the teenage girl, who sat and glared at the floor. "What room is he in?"

"Room 547. Please, go see him."

Aliyah nodded and headed in that direction. She didn't know what to expect. The last photographic memory of her father was from the night he left her and her mother. Her anxiety multiplied as she passed by each room. Each one brought her closer to the man she swore to hate yet so desperately wanted to love her.

She reached the room and stalled. She tried to convince herself the pain of her youth no longer existed, that she wasn't a twenty-seven-year-old woman suffering from her father's abandonment. Now, more than ever, she realized that was a lie.

As she pushed the door open, her feet struggled to move. She blew out a breath and walked inside. Aliyah paused and took in her father's condition. Waves of emotions rippled through her. He was no longer the six-foot-two teddy bear that gave her bear hugs as a kid. He was simply a shell of that man.

"Dad?"

Aliyah moved closer until she stood by the side of the bed. Her father's eyes were closed, and his breathing was unlabored. She picked up his hand and held it. A tear fell as she remembered how her little hand once fit inside his.

"I'm here, dad."

His hand twitched, but his eyes didn't open.

Aliyah looked around the room. She pulled the

chair she spotted in the corner over to the bed. As she sat, she picked his hand back up. She wasn't sure if her father was in a coma or a deep sleep, but she talked, anyway.

"I've missed you so much. I'm sorry I was so stubborn. If I could go back, I would." She laid her head down on the bed next to his hand.

"Moon pie."

Aliyah lifted her head and studied her father's face. "Dad?"

"Moon pie," he repeated the nickname he'd given her as a child.

She smiled at the recollection of her love for the snack cakes. She couldn't remember the last time she'd had one. "I'm here."

Cornelius's eyes fluttered and opened slowly. He swallowed and turned his head toward the sound of her voice. "Hi."

"Hi, dad." Her voice cracked as she spoke.

"Don't cry, Moon pie."

But Aliyah couldn't stop the tears. They were from years of pain and sorrow.

"I remember when you were three. You sneaked up into the kitchen cabinet and devoured an entire box of those things. When your mother found you, marshmallows and chocolate were everywhere. In your hair, your clothes, even your nose."

Aliyah laughed softly and used her hands to wipe

her face.

"Do you still eat them?"

"No, I don't. I must have eaten too many when I was little."

"What about *Whitney Houston*? Do you still listen to her? She was always your favorite."

"How did you know that? Did mom tell you?"

"No. When you were little, I used to sing '*The Greatest Love of All*' to you."

"You did?"

"Yes. You loved that song so much; you made us buy you every album *Whitney Houston* made."

All this time, she had been holding on to their memory and never knew. "I'm sorry."

"For what?" Cornelius asked.

She wiped her face again. "I thought you left because you didn't want us anymore. Mom told me the truth."

"It's not all your mom's fault. We both were to blame for the demise of our marriage. I'm so sorry you got caught in the middle."

Aliyah caressed his hand, which held hers.

"Have you met your sister?"

"No, but I saw her sitting outside in the waiting area. How old is she?"

"Fourteen."

"She's pretty."

"You both are."

"What's her name?"

"Jordan. I want you girls to become close."

Aliyah nodded.

"She's not as strong as you. She's going to need her big sister to help her through life."

"I'll be there, but she'll also have her mom and you."

"I won't always be here."

"You say that like you're leaving or something."

Cornelius forced a smile. "I'm on borrowed time."

Borrowed time. Her mother had used the words earlier.

"We all are," Cornelius continued.

Aliyah thought about that. Tomorrow wasn't promised. Any animosity she had toward her father and his wife, she had to let it go.

Cornelius's IV beeped.

"I better find the nurse. I'll be right back, dad." Aliyah bent over and kissed his cheek. As she moved to pull away, Cornelius held on to her hand.

"I love you, Aliyah. No matter what, I never stopped. I should have reached out sooner. Will you forgive me?"

"Yes, dad. I forgive you." She kissed his cheek again, and this time Cornelius let her leave.

Once in the hall, Aliyah walked to the nurse's station. "Hi, my dad's IV is beeping. He's in room 54 —"

Beep beep beep beep beep beep beep...

"Code blue, room 547! Code blue, room 547!" A woman's voice over the intercom system repeated the message.

Aliyah's eyes widened. She spun around as multiple people entered her father's room.

"Dad!" Aliyah ran toward the room, but hospital personnel intercepted her.

"Please, let us help him. I know you want to go in there, but it's best if you stay out here."

"Aliyah!"

She turned to see Stephanie and Jordan running full speed toward her. The tears streaming down her face caused them to weep as well. As they waited to be told what they already knew, the three of them held each other tight.

Chapter Seventeen

The last week had gone by in a blur. First, there was Aliyah's father's heartbreaking viewing, followed by the more painful funeral. As Aliyah helped Stephanie with the repast, she recalled the last funeral she attended. It had been her grandmother on her mom's side. Aliyah was in high school at the time and had trouble accepting her Kupuna wahine's death.

"Thank you," a woman said as Aliyah handed her a piece of cake.

Most of the people there, Aliyah, had only met days ago. At the funeral, her father's sister Angie sat behind Aliyah. She and her mother had never been close to her. From the looks of things, the woman hadn't bothered to build a relationship with Stephanie and Jordan, either.

Through the living-room window, Aliyah spotted

Jordan. She sat alone on the front porch swing. A couple of seconds went by, then someone came over and gave their condolences. Aliyah could tell their words had done little to help. Despite her pain, she knew their father's death hurt Jordan the most.

As though she heard her sister's call, Aliyah moved toward the front of the house. When she stepped onto the porch, Jordan turned her head.

"Hi, can I join you?"

Jordan nodded.

Aliyah walked toward the swing and noticed the tears on Jordan's cheek. She sat next to her, and they both stared straight ahead.

"I miss him," Jordan said.

"Me too."

"Are you going to disappear after today?"

Aliyah looked at Jordan. "Do you want me to?"

She shook her head and met Aliyah's gaze. "No, I don't."

"Then I won't." Aliyah smiled and squeezed Jordan's hand. At that moment, she understood why her father had been reaching out. He knew he had little time left. No matter the circumstances, Jordan needed her, and Aliyah would not let her or their father down.

"Thank you, Aliyah. You're a Godsend." Stephanie said. "My sister can't fly here until next week. This whole dreadful situation has happened so fast." She shook her head, and tears spilled from her eyes.

Aliyah dried the last plate and stuck the dish inside the cabinet. She walked over to Stephanie and hugged her.

"I'm such a mess."

"You're allowed to be a mess."

Stephanie chuckled and used a napkin to dab at her eyes. "I would have never guessed you'd be here, helping me."

"I know. This is all beyond me, too."

"There's something I've wanted to say to you for a long time." Stephanie sat at the kitchen table. "Please, have a seat."

Aliyah squinted and sat in the chair across from her.

"I'm sorry for what I did—to you and your mom. I knew your father was married. I figured the only way he'd leave your mother was if I got pregnant."

To hear Stephanie admit what she'd done made Aliyah's stomach turn.

"There was also the possibility Cornelius wasn't your father. I used that to my advantage. I was young and selfish." Stephanie stared at the floor. "I'm ashamed to have someone I deliberately hurt be my only source of support."

Through closed eyes, Aliyah willed her anger

away. She thought about Ethan's words and repeated them. "Sometimes, it's not about who's right. It's about doing the right thing." She'd held so much hate for the woman before her, even more toward the girl upstairs. Aliyah refused to carry that burden anymore. "I forgive you."

Stephanie wiped the tears from her face and nodded.

With a heavy heart, Aliyah took a deep breath. "It's late. I better go."

"We have a guest room. You're welcome to stay. I'm sure Jordan would love to see your face in the morning."

At the mention of her little sister, Aliyah decided she'd stay. "Sure, why not?" She pulled on the formal black dress she wore. "I might have to borrow some clothes, though."

February~

Ethan had tried calling. He'd sent text messages and multiple emails, but Aliyah never responded. Out of respect, he decided not to make a spectacle of things at Mills, but that hadn't stopped him from showing up at her house every so often—not that it did any good. Each time he showed up, Aliyah ignored him.

A month. That's how long it had been since his life went to shit. Like Kimberly predicted, Hillary slithered her way back and fucked up his world.

Ethan shifted the papers in front of him. The words ran together; he couldn't focus or concentrate anymore. In his hand, he rotated the stress balls faster. They weren't doing him any good. The entire time he held them, he'd been contemplating throwing them across the room.

In five hours, he would board his private jet en route to Paris. Aliyah was supposed to accompany him, but—because of his stupidity—she hated him.

Ethan set the balls down and palmed his face. He wanted to see his little brother, but he'd particularly planned an extraordinary trip for Aliyah. Since this would have been her first time there, he wanted to make it memorable.

"Shit!" Unable to resist the urge any longer, Ethan hurled one of the stress balls across the room toward the door.

"What the hell is going on in here?" A startled Xavier entered the office, following the sound of the heavy ball hitting the wooden door. After inspecting the dent, he picked up the ball.

"What do you want?"

Xavier ignored Ethan's grumpy state and sat in

the seat in front of the desk. "It's been a couple of days since I heard from you. Are you still going to Paris?"

"I've been busy, and yes, I am."

Xavier nodded. "So, how's it going?"

Ethan glared at Xavier through hooded eyes. "Peachy."

"Listen—"

"Spare me!"

"I was going to say I'm here if you need anything."

Heart-felt emotions and communication were not strengths Ethan possessed. No one knew that better than Xavier. "Thanks, but I'm fine."

With another nod, Xavier stood. "Well, I'm going to head out. Tell Alex I said hello." He gave Ethan a once over, then left.

It wasn't Xavier's fault. However, Ethan wasn't in the mood for deep conversations that led to the revelation he was his own worst enemy.

Ethan relaxed his shoulders and leaned back in his chair. There was no telling how long he'd be gone. At one point, he'd thought about canceling the trip and rescheduling. But with the way things were between him and Aliyah, Ethan needed to leave Seattle for a while.

For once, he felt something for someone other than a sexual desire. For once, he thought about a tomorrow with someone by his side. His short-lived marriage to Hillary had been out of obligation, not love.

Love. The word echoed in his head. Did he love Aliyah? *Yes.* He'd become a disoriented fool since the day she walked out. Despite all his possessions, he had nothing.

Ethan picked up his phone to call Michael, then resolved to head over there instead. Since the incident, he conducted all communication regarding Cedar Peak through him. Production of the resort started in two months. They were right on schedule.

Ethan wondered if Aliyah still involved herself with his account. With little effort, he swallowed the last of his pride and tried once more to get through to her.

As he reached for a pen and a sheet of paper, he thought of the letter he'd written her in Montego Bay. At that moment, nothing but the desire to devour her mattered to him. Now, Ethan needed much more from Aliyah. He needed her companionship and her presence in his life.

He wrote a few lines, then crumbled the paper and tossed it to the floor. Simple, he thought as he wrote again.

At a quarter to four, Ethan entered Mills and headed to Michael's office.

"Enjoy your trip. Don't worry about Cedar Peak. I promise not to disturb you unless it's a dire need."

"Thank you." Ethan's movements were slow as he pulled Aliyah's letter from inside his blazer's pocket.

"What's this?" Michael eyed the closed envelope Ethan handed him.

"I need you to give that to Aliyah for me."

"Are you sure you don't want to give this to her yourself?"

"I doubt she'd let me within ten feet of her."

"She might."

Ethan squinted and tilted his head to the side.

"She's going to kill me for telling you this, but her father passed away four weeks ago."

Ethan mentally calculated the time. He remembered the conversation he and Aliyah had about her father.

"They amended their relationship before he died. I think it helped her—with everything," Michael said.

"Thanks for sharing that with me. Maybe I'll call her once I land in Paris."

Michael nodded. "I'll make sure she gets this. As I said, don't worry about Cedar Peak. I'll keep you in the loop."

Ethan turned to leave, but spun back around. "Who's the new project manager?"

"Come again?"

"The new project manager over Cedar Peak. With all that's transpired, I figured Aliyah would have wanted to be removed from my account." Ethan wasn't sure how much Michael knew, but considering how close they were, he was certain he knew enough.

"She didn't," Michael said.

Intrigue flashed on Ethan's face. Was there hope? Or was she being professional? Ethan leaned toward the latter as he walked out of Michael's office.

*K*nocks on her door made Aliyah glance away from the computer screen. "Hey, what's up?"

"Ethan stopped by," Michael informed her.

"What did he want?"

"He's leaving for Paris. He wanted me to give you this." Michael handed her the letter.

With her father's passing still fresh in her mind, she had forgotten about Paris. A week had gone by since Ethan tried to reach her. "Is he still here?" Aliyah asked, as she flipped over the unopened envelope.

"No, he—"

"Well, well, well."

Aliyah and Michael looked toward the doorway. Tina stood there with a sly smile.

"We'll talk later," Michael said with irritation. He walked toward Tina and attempted to leave. "Excuse me, Tina."

"That's it? No hello?"

"Hello, Tina. How are you?"

"Great! What about you?"

"Even better. Now, if you'll excuse me."

After a second or two, Tina stepped to the side and let Michael pass.

Aliyah glared at Tina. "That was unnecessary."

"What? I was trying to be friendly." She walked over to Aliyah's desk. "It doesn't matter, anyway. I'm officially off the market." Tina held out her hand and showed off her massive engagement ring.

"Wow! Ben did the damn thing."

"Yes, he did!" Tina squealed with delight.

"Is that why you're here? To show off your huge rock and rub it in my face?"

"Yes, and no. I came to take my maid of honor to lunch."

Aliyah's eyes widened as she smiled. "Maid of honor?"

"Yes. You're the reason Ben and I are back together."

"Aww, thanks, hun. So, which freak em dress was

it?"

"The red one."

More knocks came at the door.

"My office is Grand Central Station today," Aliyah said.

"Sorry, I didn't know you had company. Do you want me to come back?"

"Oh, no. You're okay, Danita. Please, come in."

The change in Tina's body language hadn't gone ignored by Aliyah. She gave her the eye and mouthed, "Don't!"

"I need a couple of signatures, and I'll be out of your hair." Danita smiled at Tina. "Hi."

"Hi, I'm Tina. Aliyah's close friend."

Aliyah rolled her eyes. For Danita's protection, she had to get rid of her fast. "Here you go. All done."

"Thanks." Danita picked up the folder and headed out.

"Aliyah and I are about to go to lunch. Would you like to join us?"

Aliyah prayed Danita wouldn't accept Tina's invitation, especially since she had an ulterior motive for asking.

"No thanks. My boyfriend cooked lasagna last night. I brought some in for lunch today."

Aliyah wanted to laugh. She pressed her lips together and waited for Danita to leave.

"My boyfriend cooked lasagna," Tina mimicked

in a condescending tone. "Since when is Michael so domestic?"

"Stop. Besides, you asked for it," Aliyah reminded. She grabbed her purse and led the way to the elevator.

Over lunch, Aliyah listened as Tina talked about the who, what, when, why, and how of her wedding. For someone who claimed not to be ready five months ago, she had done a complete one-eighty.

"Hey?"

"Yeah."

"Have you heard from Ethan?"

Aliyah thought about the unopened envelope on her desk. "He left for Paris today."

"I'm sorry, Liya. I know how much you liked him. You should call him."

"I can't."

"Why not?"

"He gave Michael a letter to give to me before he left."

"Oh? What did it say?"

"I haven't read it yet. I'm not sure if I want to." Aliyah shrugged. "I'm not ready to read what I already know."

"Such as?"

Aliyah picked up a napkin and wiped her mouth. "That he's sorry and how he wishes things were different. That he won't try to contact me anymore."

Tina reached for Aliyah's hand. "You're going to get through this, friend. In the meantime, how about a lingerie party?"

"A what?" Aliyah scrunched her brows.

"Lingerie party. It's like a Tupperware party only with lingerie."

Aliyah didn't know how Tina came up with some of her ideas, but this was out of the box. "Where exactly would we host this party?"

"Your house."

"Of course," Aliyah replied dryly. Her house was always the destination when Tina planned any event.

"Leave the details up to me. I'll let you know when."

Aliyah bit into her sandwich and gave an unenthused nod.

Chapter Eighteen

March~

Another month passed, and Ethan still hadn't received a response from Aliyah. He wasn't sure what to expect. Had she read the letter and decided she didn't care? Maybe she never read the letter and simply tossed it in the trash.

At seven o'clock in the evening, Ethan and Alex were still working. Winter and spring were the hotel's busiest seasons. Although Ethan knew Alex could handle the load, he enjoyed working side by side with his brother.

"All right, I've tried not to pry long enough. What happened?" Alex stared at Ethan and waited for a response.

"What are you talking about?"

"I'm talking about the lame-ass excuse you gave why Aliyah didn't come with you."

Ethan pushed back from the desk and stood. He walked over to the window and peered through the rain. "Hillary happened."

Alex closed his eyes and lowered his head.

"I didn't tell her about Hillary. She showed up at my place while Aliyah was there—and this is Hillary we're talking about—so I'm sure you don't need all the nasty details."

"Then it's over between you and Aliyah?"

Ethan delayed his response, choosing to focus on the person running in the rain down below. "That's the way it seems."

"Damn, I'm sorry. The last time we talked, you were so excited. I kind of..."

Ethan faced Alex. "You kind of what?"

"Got a little jealous of your relationship."

"Why?"

"Out of the two of us, you're not the one I thought would find love first."

Ethan turned around and stared out the window once more.

"You should call her," Alex urged.

Ethan considered Alex's advice. Michael was out of town, which would force Aliyah to take his call. If that were the only way for them to communicate, he would rather they didn't.

*A*nother day, another dollar. Aliyah thought of the old saying her father often repeated. Since his passing, she'd thought about him more than usual. Thankfully, only the positive memories prevailed. Aliyah hated that her stubbornness had denied her valuable time with him. She wasn't to blame as a child, but she had been judgmental and assumed so much as an adult.

Good people do bad things. A fact even she was guilty of.

Call him.

Aliyah's conscience nagged at her for the past two days to call Ethan. A month had gone by since he'd left for Paris, and she still hadn't opened his letter. When she learned Michael had to attend a conference, she became edgy. The buffer between her and Ethan ceased to exist. Perhaps she didn't need one. Ethan hadn't tried to contact her in over a month.

Beep, Beep. Beep, Beep.

Aliyah answered her direct line. "This is Aliyah."

"Hey, it's Cecil. I got some housekeeping things I need to run by you."

Disappointment and relief swept over Aliyah.

Despite her reservations, she wanted the caller to be Ethan.

"What's wrong?" Aliyah and Cecil worked on many projects together. If he bothered to reach out, something important had come up that required her approval.

"We have a slight issue with pricing regarding the materials we need for the Phillips project."

Aliyah pulled out her notepad and scribbled the different options and new prices. "Thanks, Cecil. I'll notify Mr. Phillips and let you know how to proceed."

As she replaced the phone on the receiver, fear swelled in Aliyah's chest. Almost instantly, her palms became sweaty, and her heart raced like a horse at the Kentucky Derby. *What if he asks about the letter?* Aliyah's eyes darted downward as she pulled the drawer to her desk open. From inside, she retrieved the envelope and opened Ethan's letter.

Aliyah,
I'm sorry.
These are two words I have rarely used. I say that not to be arrogant, but hoping you will understand how truly sorry I am for hurting you. I had my reasons for not telling you about Hillary. But I never meant to deceive you, only protect you. Even though I hate discussing her, I should have told you the truth.

When you're ready to listen, I'll be here. If you decide otherwise, I understand. Just know I love you, Buttercup.

Ethan.

Aliyah blew out a breath and extended her shaky hand toward her cell phone. With eagerness, she waited for Ethan to pick up.

"Hello,"

The male voice that came through the other end didn't possess the deepness Aliyah recognized. She chalked it up to the time they'd spent apart and decided she would say her piece.

"I'm sure I handled this wrong. You deserve a chance to explain. I owe you that. So, if you still want to talk, I'm ready to listen."

"Aliyah, this is Alex. Ethan had to step out for a second. He left his phone, but he'll be right back."

"Oh." Aliyah's face flushed with heat.

"How are you?" Alex asked.

"I'm good. I need Ethan to approve a price change before we can proceed," she explained, as though Alex hadn't heard her previous babble.

"Speak of the devil. Here he is now."

Aliyah heard Ethan ask Alex who was on the phone. Another second passed, and Ethan's voice came through the receiver.

"Hey."

"Hi. There's, there's an issue—a price change for the materials. Because of the amount, I have to run it by you."

"How much?"

"If we want to stay on schedule, it's going to cost ninety-thousand more. There's a cheaper option, but we'll fall a week behind."

"I think you know which one I prefer."

"Right. I'll approve the ninety-thousand."

"Is there anything else?"

Minutes ago, it had been so easy to say what she needed to say. Now, Aliyah felt put on the spot. "Yes, there is. I read your letter, and I'm ready to listen."

When Ethan sighed, Aliyah wasn't sure how to interpret. She patiently waited for him to respond.

"I didn't want to expose you to her."

"Meaning?"

"Hillary and I have a long history. Our fathers were business partners, and our families were close. We fooled around, but we were never exclusive."

Aliyah remained quiet.

"At the beginning of last year—after one of our hookups—she got pregnant. We've always used protection, including that night, but the condom broke. A month later, she showed me a sonogram. She claimed she hadn't slept with anyone else and that I was the father."

Does he have a child? Aliyah shifted in her chair and

moved the phone to her other ear.

"Out of respect for our parents' friendship and her dying father, I married her," he confessed.

"What about love? Didn't you love her?"

Ethan fell silent for a moment, then spoke again. "My dad raised me to be a man and take care of my responsibilities."

"So, out of duty, you married her?"

"Yes."

"Why did you get a divorce?"

"Three months into our marriage, I came back from a business trip to find my house full of people I didn't know. I spotted Hillary among her friends, drunk."

At once, Aliyah thought about the unborn baby.

"I dragged her into the other room. I asked her what in the hell she was thinking. She laughed hysterically and told me she had killed the baby weeks prior."

"Oh, my God!"

"I lost control. If it weren't for her friends, prying my hands from around her neck, I might have killed Hillary that night."

Tears fell down Aliyah's cheek.

"I left and filed for divorce the next day. The fact she used the baby to trick me and then killed it, was pure evil."

"Ethan, I'm sorry you went through that."

"In September, as part of our divorce settlement, I bought her shares for Taylor & Hensworth. After that, I figured she was out of my life for good."

"When we met in Montego Bay, you were going through a divorce?"

"Yes, and I never thought I would see you again; I didn't think you needed to know. But then, I found you in Seattle. I should have told you before I let things go so far with us. I'm sorry for the pain I caused you. Can you forgive me?"

"Yes, I forgive you."

Ethan exhaled. "I miss you, Buttercup."

"I miss you too. When are you coming home?"

"Next month."

"For Cedar Peak's ground-breaking?"

"Yeah, but I can come back sooner. I'm sure Alex wants me gone."

"I doubt he wants you to leave. I'll just have to wait."

"Are you sure?"

"Yes, no."

Ethan chuckled. "I love you, Buttercup."

"I love you too." She finally admitted to him and herself. There was no turning back.

"Now that my life has meaning again, I want to know what you've been up to," Ethan said.

Over the next hour, Aliyah told Ethan about her father's passing, her new relationship with his wife, and her half-sister. She enjoyed their talk and the peace it gave her.

As the days passed, the miles between her and Ethan had become a hard pill to swallow. Despite the beautiful pink and red roses that filled her living room, Aliyah craved him more. Like a love-struck teen, she read the card that accompanied the roses again.

Soon, Buttercup. I can't wait to hold you.

Forever yours,
Ethan

Aliyah marked down the days for Ethan's return on her kitchen calendar. Two weeks, that's how long she had to wait. With a big smile, she headed upstairs to her bedroom to get dressed. She was taking Jordan shopping and to lunch.

In the beginning, the promise she made to her father had been her only motive. However, she no longer blamed Stephanie and Jordan for her parent's divorce or the end of her relationship with her father.

These days, they were both a welcoming necessity in Aliyah's life.

After a short drive, Aliyah arrived at Stephanie and Jordan's subdivision. She turned off her car and headed toward the front steps of the white two-story craftsman home. The house belonged in a *Better Homes and Gardens* magazine with its perfectly manicured lawn, colorful flower garden, and bird fountain. By the front door, she pressed the doorbell, and a whimsical melody played as she waited.

"Aliyah, come on in." Stephanie welcomed her with a hug.

"How are you today?" Aliyah asked once inside. Since her father's death, they made a point of checking on each other's mental state.

"Today's a good day. What about you?"

"It's a good day for me, too." With empathy, Aliyah smiled.

"What do you girls have planned?"

"Lunch and a little shopping."

"Liya!" Jordan called out as she ran down the stairs.

"Hey!"

"Guess what!"

From her vast grin, Aliyah gathered the extra study sessions had paid off. "What?"

"I got an 'A' on my math test, and I owe it to you!"

"I'm so glad I could help. Math was my best subject in school."

"Like your father," Stephanie mentioned.

"Yeah, dad loved math." Aliyah smiled warmly at Jordan. "Come on, let's go celebrate. Stephanie, do you want to come with us?"

"No, you girls enjoy yourselves."

"Bye, mom." Jordan crossed the room and kissed Stephanie on the cheek.

"Can we at least bring you something back?" Aliyah asked.

"Sure. I'll take a cinnamon bun."

Aliyah nodded, then headed out with Jordan in tow.

As they drove, Aliyah wondered if she should have insisted Stephanie come with them. Although she claimed to be fine, Aliyah wasn't sure if that was the case anymore. Her demeanor significantly changed after she spoke about Aliyah's father. She didn't want to pry or push. Her relationship with Jordan and Stephanie was still a work in progress.

"So, kiddo, any exciting things to talk about."

"You mean, Brad?"

Aliyah laughed. "Yes … Come on. You know I live for your stories."

"We talked."

"What!" Aliyah glanced at Jordan. "Who made

the first move?"

"He did."

"I told you he likes you."

Jordan's face lit up with excitement. "We have a project together. He didn't exactly have a choice."

"Hey, don't downplay the situation. Baby steps, you know," Aliyah told her.

Jordan exhaled deeply. "I become so nervous when I'm around him. Like I can't breathe or think straight."

Aliyah thought about her first crush, Kevin. He was a senior, and she was a freshman. Her anxiety always kicked into high gear whenever they were in the same room. She remembered the time she threw up because he spoke to her. Aliyah cringed on the inside.

She certainly wasn't the same insecure girl anymore, but she could still relate. "It'll get better. I promise."

Since shopping always cheered Aliyah up, she suspected a little retail therapy would also brighten Jordan's mood. After splurging in various stores, they headed to the food court for lunch. Aliyah settled on a grilled chicken Caesar salad, and Jordan chose a slice of cheese pizza. While they ate, Jordan talked more about school, and Aliyah shared her high school memories.

"Ready to go?"

"Yeah," Jordan said. "I don't think we have enough hands to carry any more bags."

"I believe you're right. Let's buy your mom a cinnamon bun first." Aliyah handed Jordan ten dollars, and she headed over to the bakery.

As she waited for Jordan to return, Aliyah's phone vibrated against the table. She slid the green button and answered Tina's call.

"Hey."

"Do you remember the lingerie party we talked about?"

"Yeah, what about it?"

"We're going to have it tonight."

"Tonight?"

"Yeah. Are you busy or something?—I know you're not. Ethan is still in Paris.... Hello? Aliyah?"

"I'm giving you the finger."

"Cute," Tina retorted.

"I'm out with my little sister right now, but I should be home within an hour." Aliyah had forgotten to ask the most important question when she agreed to allow this party to take place at her house. "Exactly how many people are we talking about?"

"Ten. With me, you, Serena, Amanda, and Terry—the host—included."

"What time is this little shindig supposed to

start?"

"Six o'clock."

"After I drop Jordan off, I'll head home. Give Terry my address and phone number."

"Thanks, Liya."

"You're welcome. Text me when you're on the way." Aliyah pulled the phone from her ear, but placed it back when she heard Tina call her name. "Is there something else?"

"Yeah. Could you pick up some wine?"

"Sure. Is that it?" She regretted the question the second she asked.

"Order some pizza too," Tina added.

"Fine!"

"I really appreciate this, Liya."

"Uh-huh."

"I'll dance at your wedding."

"Yeah, yeah."

Tina gasped.

"What's wrong now?"

"You said yeah, yeah."

Aliyah raised her brow. "What's your point?"

"Usually, you go ballistic when I mention the idea of you and marriage in the same sentence."

"Are we done here?"

"You're thinking about marrying Ethan, aren't you?"

"No! We've been dating for less than a year. Why

would I be thinking about marriage?"

"Maybe not today or next month, but the thought is in the back of your head."

"Tina!"

"Fine, I'll drop the subject for now."

As Aliyah hung up, she thought about Tina's question. Marriage *was* in the back of her mind. She and Ethan had discussed their feelings regarding the matter, with him being for it and her against it.

Aliyah wasn't sure if she still felt that way. She was also unsure if she could devote time and energy to a big wedding only to have the marriage fizzle out years down the road? What if he stopped loving her? What if she stopped loving him? Marriage was such a gamble. You invest everything, with the possibility of being left with nothing.

Aliyah noticed Jordan on her way back and quickly removed the pained expression from her face.

Chapter Nineteen

In the grocery store's parking lot, Aliyah sat inside her car. She glanced at her phone and contemplated if she should call Ethan. They'd spoken the night before but hadn't talked at all that day. Although it was Saturday, she knew he'd gone into work early and likely worked late.

Like her, Ethan worked a hectic schedule, often putting his business first. She wondered if either of them had what it took to make a marriage work. Then she thought about the time they'd spent together before Ethan went to Paris. Somehow, they found a way.

Aliyah closed her eyes and exhaled. She was stressing about something that wasn't even an issue. "It's not like the man proposed."

Inside the grocery store, she knew exactly where to find the wine. After grabbing two bottles of Pinot Grigio and two bottles of Chardonnay, she started toward the register.

"Hey there, stranger."

Aliyah turned her head. At the sight of the man in front of her, she nearly dropped the bottles in her hand. He wasn't alone, either. *Retreat.* Doing so, she headed in the opposite direction.

"Wait! Please!"

Hesitantly, Aliyah turned around.

"Go wait for me in the car," Lorenzo told the woman who was not his wife.

Aliyah's eyes followed as she disappeared down the aisle. "You're unbelievable."

Lorenzo looked away.

"Does she know that you're married?"

"No."

Once again, Aliyah turned to leave.

"I'm sorry!" he blurted, halting her steps. "I should have told you I was married. Things between Amy and I aren't good."

Aliyah remained quiet as she faced him.

"I fell for you," Lorenzo professed. "Everything I said, I meant, Aliyah. I still love you."

"What about your wife, huh? Better yet, your unborn child and your daughter?" Aliyah gripped the bottles of wine she held tighter. "Men like you turn women into bitter versions of themselves. You make us believe we're incapable of receiving anything better than the *so-called* love you give."

"You hate me, don't you?" Lorenzo asked.

"No, not anymore. I made peace with this—with us. I feel nothing for you." Aliyah turned to leave, but faced Lorenzo once more. "Your wife deserves better. Cheating on her won't fix whatever problems you *claim* to have."

Aliyah didn't wait for a response. She walked off the aisle and headed to the register. No more would she live in the past. No more would she give things she couldn't control power over her life.

It was five o'clock, almost time for the girls to show up. After paying for the pizza and tipping the delivery guy, Aliyah texted Ethan. He was probably asleep, considering it was 2 AM in Paris. She became angry with herself that she hadn't called him earlier.

Aliyah:
I Can't wait until you come home. 14 days to go.
Delivered: 5:01 PM

She waited eagerly for a response. When Ethan didn't, she figured her assumption he was asleep had been accurate.

Ding!

Aliyah's heartbeat quickened with joy, then dismay. The notification came from Amanda, followed by one from Serena and Tina. They were all giving Aliyah updates on their arrival times. She texted them back, then joined Terry in the living room to help finish with the setup.

An hour later, Terry had transformed Aliyah's living room into a *Victoria's Secret* lingerie show. Laughter spilled out while *Mary Jane Girls 'All Night Long'* played in the background.

"Oh, I love that one!" Amanda eyed the purple teddy Serena held under her chin.

"Here, do you want it? This *is* your favorite color," Serena said as she handed the lingerie over to her.

"It's Ashton's favorite color too. At least on me."

"Ben loves when I wear red," Tina said as she walked toward the stand-up mirror wearing a two-piece negligee.

"I hope you're buying that cause I'm not putting that anywhere near my body after you've had it all up in your twat," Amanda said.

"I look too good, not too." Tina turned to the side and made her ass cheeks jiggle.

"Excuse me, but this is not a twerk show," Amanda reprimanded.

"You're just jealous because you can't do it."

Amanda stood and tossed the garment she held on the sofa. Without a word, she twerked effortlessly.

Not the one to be outdone, Tina retaliated by dropping to her knees and making her ass cheeks jump again.

Aliyah and everyone else broke out into a hysterical frenzy. They reached for their purses and pulled out money to throw on both women.

"This is by far my best lingerie party. You girls are definitely my favorite customers," Terry said as she pulled money from her purse and joined the others.

Ethan smiled as he read and responded to Aliyah's text.

Ethan:
I can't wait to come home. 13 days to go.
Delivered: 6:05 AM

Ding!

Ethan thought Aliyah would be asleep. He hadn't expected her to text back.

Aliyah:
13 days to go, Mr. Phillips.
I have a lot of naughty things planned for you.
Received: 6:06 AM

Ethan wasn't sure what had gotten into her, but he liked where their conversation was going. He dialed Aliyah's number, needing to hear her voice.

"Hey, baby," she purred through the phone.

Baby? Ethan glanced at his phone. "Aliyah, have you been drinking?"

"A little."

"Where are you?" he asked with concern.

"Home, in my bed. Where you should be."

"Is that so?"

"Yep."

Oh, yeah. His woman was tipsy. "What exactly would we do if I were there?"

"Hmm. For starters, I would completely undress you. Then, I would tie you up—give you a dose of your own medicine."

Ethan chuckled.

"I'd undress, leaving only my panties on."

A groan of torment eased from Ethan's throat as he pictured Aliyah in nothing but one of her lace thongs.

"While you lie there helpless and incapacitated, I would slide down that sexy body of yours, all the way to your big, long, thick, rock-hard cock."

Cock! Ethan bit his fist. He'd never heard Aliyah use that word. When they had sex, she wasn't afraid to express her enjoyment, but never had she said that word. "And what would you do with my cock?"

"Lick it. I'd get the tip nice and wet before I slid you to the back of my throat."

Ethan shifted in bed. His dick had already sprung to life when her voice came through the phone. "Damn, all the way to the back?"

"Yes! Then, after I've made you cum—using only my mouth—I'd swallow every delicious drop." Aliyah taunted.

"Fuck." Ethan groaned as he stroked himself.

"You like that?" Aliyah whispered.

"Yes, fuck yes!"

"Good, cause I'm not done."

"You're not?" Ethan moistened his lips.

"Nope. Next, I would straddle you. Inch by inch, I would ease you inside me. I'd grind slowly, making sure you filled me completely."

Ethan gripped his engorged shaft.

"Can you feel me, baby?" Aliyah asked.

"Yes!"

"Should I move faster?"

"Yes!" Ethan answered with delayed speech as his hand pumped more rapidly.

"How's that? Is it good?"

When Aliyah moaned, Ethan knew she was taking care of herself while getting him off. "Oh, shit! I'm about to cum!" Ethan shouted, unable to keep his voice down.

"Me too! Give it to me, baby!"

Ropes of cum shot out as his body tensed and his back arched. On the other end of the phone, he heard Aliyah gasp as she succumbed to her orgasm.

"Wow! Baby, that was incredible."

Ethan sat up when she didn't respond. "Buttercup?"

Soft breathing, followed by light snores, traveled through the phone into Ethan's ear. He laughed and shook his head. "I love you, woman. Goodnight, Buttercup." Ethan hung up and stared at the ceiling. It was time to go home. But first, he needed to find her a special gift. One that showed how much she meant to him.

Ethan jumped out of bed. He remembered the cum on his leg and hurried toward the bathroom.

Around noon, Ethan emerged from Alex's spare bedroom. In the kitchen, he searched the fridge for something to drink and settled on a bottle of water.

"Where is she?"

Ethan turned around to find Alex on the opposite side of the kitchen island. "Who?"

"Aliyah. Isn't she here? With all the noise you made this morning, I thought she flew in during the night."

"Still a perv, I see."

"Whatever. If you weren't so loud, I wouldn't have heard anything."

Ethan tossed the water bottle top at Alex. "I need your help."

"With what?"

"I want to buy Aliyah something special."

"Thanking her for the morning nut, are we?" When Ethan motioned to throw the water on him, Alex raised his hands in defense. "I'm joking! I'm glad the two of you are working things out."

Ethan lowered the bottle. "That's why I want to get her something special."

"Like, I love you special?"

"Yeah."

"How about a promise ring?"

"A promise ring? That's for high-school kids."

"Not true. People of all ages wear promise rings."

Ethan thought about it. The more he did, the more the idea made sense. "Fuck it. A promise ring it is." He drank the rest of his water and walked over to Alex. "Put some clothes on. We're going shopping."

"Now? Today!"

"Yes."

"Why do I have to go?"

"Because it's your idea, and I said so."

Alex crossed his arms. "I'm not a kid anymore. I can kick your ass."

Ethan smirked. He looked away, then quickly turned back around and jabbed Alex in his side.

"Cheap shot!" Alex groaned.

"Get dressed," Ethan ordered again as he headed back into the spare bedroom and followed his own instructions.

*W*ith one week left before Cedar Peak's groundbreaking, Aliyah prepared for her trip to Skykomish. Ethan wasn't due back for another week, but he'd made plans for her to stay at his cabin. When Michael and Danita volunteered to stay there with her, Aliyah was glad. She'd been nervous about sleeping in the huge cabin alone.

When Todd pulled into the driveway, the breathtaking view of the luxury cabin had the same effect on her.

"Should we take the same rooms we had the last time?" Michael asked.

"Sure, if you think you'll need two."

Danita and Michael both laughed.

As Todd helped them inside, Mrs. Hansen greeted them in the entryway.

"It's so good to have you all back again."

"We're glad to be back," Aliyah said.

Michael sniffed the air. "What's that amazing smell?"

"The Shepherd's pie I baked. After you've put your things away, come into the kitchen, and I'll fix you all a plate."

The three of them nodded and headed toward the spiral staircase.

"Ms. Carter?"

"Yes." Aliyah turned around.

"Mr. Phillips had a package delivered for you."

"Oh, where?"

"Upstairs in his room." Mrs. Hansen said, then walked in the kitchen's direction.

At the top of the stairs, Aliyah went one way while Michael and Danita went the other. Aliyah knew the two planned to share a room. She chuckled on the inside because she planned to do the same. Aliyah bypassed the room she stayed in the last time and walked toward Ethan's suite. At the door, she paused when Ethan's scent surrounded her.

Tears formed the minute she turned the knob, and her eyes met his. Aliyah dropped her luggage and ran toward him.

"Hey, Buttercup." Ethan wiped her eyes and cheeks with his thumbs. "Don't cry, babe."

"I missed you."

Ethan kissed her gently on the lips. "I missed you too." He took her by the hand and guided her over to the bed. "I have something for you."

Seductively, Aliyah bit her bottom lip.

"Not that, at least not yet."

Aliyah remembered the others. "You wanted me to stay here, so we could spend time alone." She glanced at the floor. "I may have messed up your plans by bringing Michael and Danita."

Ethan sat and pulled her between his legs. "It's all right, Buttercup. I'm cool with them being here. We'll have plenty of alone time soon."

Aliyah nodded and combed her fingers through the hairs on the back of Ethan's head.

"I want to give you something before we head downstairs."

Her eyes grew large as Ethan removed a small box from his pocket. "Is that what I think it is?"

Ethan stood. "Yes, and no."

She tilted her head to the side. Her eyes glimmered with daze as he opened the box and removed the large princess-cut canary diamond.

"This is a promise ring."

"A promise ring?" she repeated.

"I promise to communicate. To never keep things from you, no matter how bad it seems. I promise to love you unconditionally, as the independent woman you are. Most of all, I promise to replace this ring with something more permanent when we're both ready. What do you say?" Ethan donned a more serious expression.

"Will you go steady with me?"

"Yes!" she said with laughter.

After securing the ring in place, Ethan kissed her again. This time with more passion.

"This is my first promise ring," Aliyah said, admiring her finger.

"Alex gave me the idea."

"Oh?" Aliyah snaked her arms around Ethan. "I'll have to give him a big hug and a kiss when I finally meet him in person."

"Well, I picked out the ring. If anyone deserves kisses and hugs, I do."

"Don't worry. I have plenty of kisses and hugs for you. Along with other ways to show my affection."

Ethan's eyes widened. "Yes, I believe we should discuss those now."

Aliyah took a step back and pushed Ethan down on the bed. "Anything to please my man."

Epilogue

Three Years Later~

Montego Bay, Jamaica

Aliyah stared at the immense Emerald-cut diamond on her finger. No longer was she Ms. Carter, but Mrs. Phillips-Taylor. In three years, so much had changed. Who knew one night would lead to her marrying the man she never knew she needed?

She eased out of the king-sized bed from under Ethan's hold, careful not to wake him. From the chase at the foot of the bed, she grabbed her white, sheer robe and headed toward the balcony. Stretched in front of her, the Caribbean Sea crashed against the shore while the silhouettes of birds flew by.

Aliyah hadn't checked the time, but the sun had yet to rise. She inhaled and closed her eyes as a gentle breeze caressed her face.

"Hey, what are you doing out here?" From behind, Ethan wrapped his arms around her and kissed the side of her head.

"I'm waiting for sunrise."

"You have another hour or more until that happens."

Aliyah turned to look up at him. "What time is it?"

"A little after five."

"Oh, I didn't know it was so early. I don't think I can go back to bed now. I'd miss the sunrise if I did." She looked back out at sea.

"If you want to watch the sunrise, then we will." Ethan turned her around and grabbed her hand.

Aliyah thought for sure he'd lead her to their bed, and they'd make love for the fourth time—in the last twenty-four hours. However, he led her across their bedroom, out the door, and downstairs to the kitchen.

As she took in Ethan's bare chest and chiseled body, she became disappointed he hadn't made love to her once more.

"What's wrong?"

Unaware she'd been pouting, Aliyah shook her head. "Nothing."

Ethan raised a brow.

"I just thought we were going to..."

"Don't worry, Buttercup. We're going to break in every inch of our new house and then some."

Aliyah's nipples tingled. Three years with Ethan, and her body still reacted this way.

"Right now, as your enthusiastic dutiful husband, I have to prepare breakfast for the upcoming sunrise you wish to see."

Over the next hour, Aliyah enjoyed the view as Ethan prepared a batch of French toast, cut up a strawberry, and made two espressos.

"Want some help?" she asked as he loaded a tray with everything they needed.

"Nope. You just sit there and look beautiful."

A few minutes passed, and he instructed her to follow him out back toward the deck.

While Ethan set the tray on the table, Aliyah noticed the sun played peek-a-boo over the horizon. She brought her attention back to him, and he'd placed a plate in front of her. French toast topped with whipped cream, strawberries, and syrup awaited.

"Looks delicious," Aliyah said.

Ethan moved his chair closer to her and cut into the French toast.

Aliyah opened her mouth and took a bite when he brought the fork to her lips. "Yummy."

"Is it? Let me have a taste." He leaned forward and sucked her bottom lip before his tongue slipped inside her mouth. "Mmm, you're right, it is." With his hand on her chin, Ethan stared into her eyes. "I want to be clear and upfront with you. I married you with every intention of loving you for the rest of my life."

The corners of Aliyah's mouth turned upward. The words he spoke three years ago were the same, yet so different. "I married you with every intention of doing the same."

At her words, Ethan's eyes flickered. "I must warn you; I'm playing for keeps, Buttercup."

Aliyah cut another piece of her French toast and brought the fork to Ethan's mouth. "So, am I, Mr. Phillips."

Ethan chuckled, then ate the bite of French toast she offered.

Aliyah's life was anything but perfect, no matter how perfect she'd tried to make it in the past. She could live with that. Everything she'd been through had brought her to that precise moment.

As the sun came up, they ate breakfast and discussed their plans for the day.

"So, what do you say?" Ethan asked, checking to see how Aliyah felt about the arrangements he'd made.

"As long as I'm with you, I don't care what we do."

Ethan raised his cup, and Aliyah followed his

lead. "To the rest of our lives, Mrs. Phillips-Taylor."
"To the rest of our lives."

The End!

Did you enjoy Aliyah and Ethan's story? Please, let me know. Leave a review or rating on Goodreads and/or Amazon. I look forward to your feedback!

About the author

M.D. Alexander is an avid reader of all genres. She writes about romance and loves coffee. She believes that true success is being happy with yourself. When she's not spending time with her family, she enjoys catching up on her favorite shows.

Message From The Author

Thank you for purchasing and reading my book. I look forward to writing more stories for you to enjoy. Feel free to email me or follow me on social media. Also, please leave a review on Amazon and/or Goodreads.

Sincerely,
M.D. Alexander.

Sign up for my Newsletter to receive notification regarding the latest release, giveaways, and more!
- ➢ *https://mailchi.mp/f8831c0e93a3/m-d-alexanders-newsletter*

Purchase other books by M.D. Alexander
- ➢ *https://amazon.com/author/alexandermd*

◆ *Novels*
Desiree's Desire
New Hearts Old Flame
Raquel's Secret

◆ *Anthology/Series*
#LIPS Volume 1
#LIPS Volume 2
#LIPS Volume 3
#LIPS Volume 1 Extended   Paperback only
#LIPS Volume 2 Extended   Paperback only
#LIPS Volume 3 Extended   Paperback only
   ** *Paperbacks contain 2 additional tales.*

Social Media/Contact info

Pinterest-
www.pinterest.com/authormdalexander/boards/

Facebook-
www.facebook.com/authorm.d.alexander19

Goodreads
www.goodreads.com/authormdalexander

Twitter-
twitter.com/AuthorMDAlexan1

Wattpad-
t.co/n2K4ATzcTG?amp=1

YouTube-
www.youtube.com/channel/UCztMDyi5OJwsDIP4De5Egqg

BookBub-
www.bookbub.com/profile/m-d-alexander

Instagram-
@m.d.alexandertheauthor

Email-
Authorm.d.alexander@gmail.com

Made in the USA
Monee, IL
08 July 2022